ISSUES THAT CONCERN YOU

Going Green

Peggy Daniels Becker, *Book Editor*

South Huntington Pub. Lib.
145 Pidgeon Hill Rd.
Huntington Sta., N.Y. 11746

GREENHAVEN PRESS
A part of Gale, Cengage Learning

GALE
CENGAGE Learning™

Detroit • New York • San Francisco • New Haven, Conn • Waterville, Maine • London

$\int 363.7$ Going

Christine Nasso, *Publisher*
Elizabeth Des Chenes, *Managing Editor*

© 2011 Greenhaven Press, a part of Gale, Cengage Learning

Gale and Greenhaven Press are registered trademarks used herein under license.

For more information, contact:
Greenhaven Press
27500 Drake Rd.
Farmington Hills, MI 48331-3535
Or you can visit our Internet site at gale.cengage.com

For product information and technology assistance, contact us at

Gale Customer Support, 1-800-877-4253
For permission to use material from this text or product, submit all requests online at www.cengage.com/permissions

Further permissions questions can be e-mailed to permissionrequest@cengage.com

Articles in Greenhaven Press anthologies are often edited for length to meet page requirements. In addition, original titles of these works are changed to clearly present the main thesis and to explicitly indicate the author's opinion. Every effort is made to ensure that Greenhaven Press accurately reflects the original intent of the authors. Every effort has been made to trace the owners of copyrighted material.

Cover image copyright illstudio, 2010. Used under license from Shutterstock.com.

LIBRARY OF CONGRESS CATALOGING-IN-PUBLICATION DATA

Going green / Peggy Daniels Becker, book editor.
    p. cm. -- (Issues that concern you)
  Includes bibliographical references and index.
  ISBN 978-0-7377-4495-8 (hardcover)
  1. Green movement. 2. Environmentalism. 3. Sustainable living. I. Becker, Peggy Daniels.
   GE195.G64 2010
   640--dc22

                                                        2010027954

Printed in the United States of America
1 2 3 4 5 6 7 14 13 12 11 10

CONTENTS

"Going green" loosely describes actions that are beneficial to the natural world, most commonly expressed with the popular slogan "reduce, reuse, recycle." Many aspects of going green are part of current public debate and discussion about issues such as global warming, energy conservation, and the "local food" movement. Making green choices can sometimes be inconvenient, expensive, or difficult to manage. And yet, many Americans continue to go out of their way to make greener choices each day. What motivates people to go green and maintain a green lifestyle over time?

Our behaviors and choices are influenced by many factors. World events, the media, our families and friends, our personal beliefs, and many other forces can combine to influence our thoughts and actions. Environmental awareness and activism have been on the rise in America for many years, as people have become more educated about potential threats to the natural world. In particular, certain large-scale environmental disasters have raised public interest and spurred Americans to go green while pressing for government action on environmental protection. Catastrophes such as the Donora "Death Fog" in Pennsylvania, the Santa Barbara oil spill in California, and the *Exxon Valdez* oil spill in Alaska caused nationwide public outrage and renewed green activism. Many current American environmental protection laws and regulations are a result of these events and the activism that followed.

The Donora "Death Fog"

One of the first events that influenced environmental lawmaking in the United States was also one of the worst air pollution disasters in the country's history. In October 1948 the town of Donora, Pennsylvania, was covered in thick smog that came to be known as the "Death Fog." An unusual weather pattern trapped toxic fumes from a nearby U.S. Steel plant over the town for four days. The polluted air killed twenty people and left hundreds more seriously ill. Experts estimated that between one-third and one-half of the town's residents were affected. It was determined that chemical emissions from the steel plant caused the deaths and illnesses.

The Donora Death Fog was an extraordinary disaster that brought the hazards of air pollution to the nation's attention. The public demanded legislation to guard against future industrial air pollution. In 1949 President Harry Truman convened the country's first national air pollution conference. Lasting anger over the Donora incident is credited with the passage of the first federal legislation on air pollution. The Air Pollution Control Act of 1955 marked the beginning of modern air pollution control efforts. Subsequently, the Clean Air Act of 1963 created a national public health program dedicated to researching techniques to monitor and control air pollution.

The Santa Barbara Oil Spill

Americans once again rallied for environmental protection after a large-scale oil spill in January 1969 in Santa Barbara, California. The underwater pipe of an offshore drilling platform operated by the Union Oil Company ruptured, releasing millions of gallons of crude oil into the Pacific Ocean. The first repairs to the ruptured pipe were successful but produced immense underground pressure that resulted in five new ruptures. The crisis continued for eleven days as workers raced to stop the spill. Ultimately, an eight-hundred-square-mile oil slick spoiled thirty-five miles of California coastline and killed hundreds of marine animals, fish, and birds. A few weeks later, underground pressure caused a new rupture that spewed even more oil for several more months.

At the time, the Santa Barbara oil spill was the worst the nation had ever seen. National news coverage fueled public anger, and environmental activism was recharged. The intensity

The January 1969 Santa Barbara oil spill caused an oil slick of eight hundred square miles, destroying thirty-five miles of California coastline and devastating the region's wildlife.

of American reactions to the spill and the related publicity is widely credited for the passage of new environmental protection laws. In January 1970 President Richard Nixon signed into law the National Environmental Policy Act.

The first Earth Day was organized on April 22, 1970, largely inspired by the Santa Barbara oil spill. Earth Day highlighted the need for environmental protection and conservation. Once again, Americans were united in environmentalism, with Earth Day drawing support from people of all walks of life and various political views. Earth Day is viewed as an influential force that helped secure passage of the Clean Air Act, the Clean Water Act, and the Endangered Species Act, all in the early 1970s. New laws were also created to strengthen offshore oil drilling regulations, and the federal Environmental Protection Agency (EPA) was formed in December 1970.

The *Exxon Valdez* Oil Spill

In March 1989 the Santa Barbara oil spill was eclipsed by a new oil disaster. While traveling from Valdez, Alaska, to Los Angeles, California, the *Exxon Valdez* oil tanker ran into the Bligh Reef in Prince William Sound. The hull of the ship was broken by the reef, and within six hours millions of gallons of crude oil gushed into the Gulf of Alaska. More than eleven hundred miles of Alaskan shoreline were contaminated by the oil spill.

Cleanup efforts were complicated by weather conditions and the remote location of the spill. Rocky shorelines and other factors made it impossible to completely remove all of the oil from the Alaskan coast. As time passed, cleanup efforts dragged on, and oil residue polluted more and more coastline. Reports and pictures of the environmental devastation were broadcast nationwide. Public anger rose, and Americans demanded that action be taken to prevent such catastrophic spills in the future. In response to public outcry, the federal government enacted strict new legislation for oil tankers, requiring that all ships be constructed with double hulls to guard against future accidental ruptures.

An Inconvenient Truth

Americans have a long history of responding to environmental crises with renewed conservation and protection efforts. Many believe the present wave of green living was spurred by the alarming statistics and forecasts presented in the award-winning 2006 documentary film *An Inconvenient Truth*. This film discusses global warming and predicts dire consequences if human habits remained unchanged. Although the extent of global warming has been hotly debated, many Americans were inspired to go green. These attitudes have been further underscored by more recent environmental disasters such as the British Petroleum

The April 21, 2010, explosion of the Deepwater Horizon oil platform in the Gulf of Mexico caused the worst environmental disaster in U.S. history.

Deepwater Horizon oil spill in the Gulf of Mexico, which began on April 20, 2010. The full extent of the damage caused by this spill has yet to be determined, but experts believe the Deepwater Horizon crisis will prove to be the worst oil spill in history.

Examining Going Green

In *Issues That Concern You: Going Green*, students will find excerpts from articles, reports, and other sources debating aspects of the green lifestyle. In addition, the volume also includes resources for further investigation. The "Organizations to Contact" section gives students direct access to organizations that are working on the issues related to going green, and the bibliography highlights recent books and periodicals for more in-depth study. The appendix "What You Should Know About Going Green" outlines basic facts and statistics, while the "What You Should Do About Going Green" section helps students use their knowledge to explore and evaluate various green practices. Taken together, these features make *Issues That Concern You: Going Green* a valuable resource for anyone researching this issue.

ONE

An Overview of Going Green

Sara Ost

> Sara Ost is a journalist whose work focuses on sustainability, design, and new media. Ost is also the editor of the EcoSalon.com Web site and newsletter. In the following viewpoint Ost gives an overview of the history of the environmental green movement in the United States. The author asserts that, while environmental sentiment can be traced back to nineteenth-century writings, the movement made a real impact on public opinion and policy with conservation programs and alarming discoveries of pollution and climate change.

The green movement as we think of it today has evolved considerably since the early days. Since there are some popular assumptions about environmental history that are incorrect, if you have an interest in green issues this article will serve as a helpful guide to the origins and evolution of "green." To understand the modern green movement, we have to trace its origins back to the beginning.

Let's get started:

While many people associate the beginning of the green movement with [biologist and nature writer] Rachel Carson's breakthrough book *Silent Spring* and the legislative fervor of the

Sara Ost, "A Brief History of the Modern Green Movement in America," WebEcoist.com, August 17, 2008. Reproduced by permission of the author.

1970s, environmentalism is in fact rooted in the intellectual thought of the 1830s and 1840s. In fact, the "environmental movement" is a significant thread in the fabric of American philosophical thought—first developed by the Transcendentalists (most famously [author and poet] Henry David Thoreau) but tangibly expanded upon during the era of American pragmatism in the latter half of the 19th century. Environmentalism isn't a trend, or a cult, or a form of hysteria. It is rooted in American philosophy and, being at once innovative and practical, idealistic and active, one could easily define modern environmentalism as quintessentially American.

Environmentalism in America today is defined [by Wikipedia .org] as: "Environmentalists advocate the sustainable management of resources and stewardship of the environment through changes in public policy and individual behavior. In its recognition of humanity as a participant in (not enemy of) ecosystems, the movement is centered on ecology, health, and human rights."

But how did we get from Thoreau and [former U.S. president] Teddy Roosevelt to "treehugging" and finally, the eco-friendly consumer-driven developments of today?

The Beginning of American Environmentalism

Rachel Carson (1907–1964) certainly helped foster a reawakening of environmentalism, but it was Henry David Thoreau, in his book *Maine Woods*, who called for the conservation of and respect for nature and the federal preservation of virgin forests.

[American diplomat] George Perkins Marsh was another key figure during the first half of the 19th century who championed preserving the natural environment. Leading intellectuals of the antebellum era called into question the standard Puritan pastoral ethic—the belief that cultivating and using the land was inherently moral and leaving the land alone to be "wild" was wasteful and uncivilized (this belief developed in large part because of the violent cultural clash between early Americans and Native Americans—something we tend to forget about in modern times). To this day there are ingrained negative associa-

American essayist and poet Henry David Thoreau (1817–1862) is considered the first conservationist. He advocated for federal government preservation of virgin forests.

tions between preserving wild lands and pantheistic or pagan values. This tension flares up in popular discourse from time to time ("environmental wackos," "treehuggers," and so forth). The classic American conflict between secular rationalism and Puritan morality is certainly not exclusive to our management of natural resources!

Though Transcendentalism [which emphasizes the individuals' understanding of a spiritual reality] was famously reverent of nature, it was the thrust of can-do American Pragmatism [which stresses that ideas are as meaningful as their practical consequences] (widely viewed to be America's original contribution to philosophical thought) that doubtless inspired a series of steps to conserve nature. Beginning in the 1860s, the United States government saw fit to create parks and set aside wild lands for public good. Yosemite was claimed in 1864 (conservationist John Muir moved there in 1869). It was made our first national park in 1872. The Audubon Society was founded in 1872, and the Sequoia and General Grant parks were established. The only setback during this era was the Mining Act of 1890, which is controversial to this day. The Forest Reserve Act finished the era of pragmatism with federal impetus. John Muir [an advocate for preservation] was elected president of the new Sierra Club in 1892.

The Conservation Movement

Though the federal government had begun taking actions to preserve lands, it was Teddy Roosevelt and John Muir—a bit of an unlikely pair—who publicized and popularized conservation. Teddy's visit to Yosemite in 1903 gained national publicity. By 1916 the National Park Service had been established with leadership by Stephen Mather [a conservationist active in politics].

But just as swiftly, the World Wars—sandwiching the traumatic Great Depression—forced environmental concerns to the background of public thought. While the Sierra Club continued to grow rapidly and became instrumental in establishing many parks during these years, environmentalism as we know it today was not a concern for most Americans—or, consequently, the federal government. It would take disasters and threats to bring environmental issues out of the organizations and ivory towers and into the mainstream again. . . .

After WWII [World War II], environmental efforts continued to be focused on conservation of land rather than more personal issues like food safety or consumer products. That soon changed. The 1948 disaster at Donora [Pennsylvania—a smog onset that killed twenty people and left thousands sick] (called the "death fog") prompted national outcry; also during this time

David Brower became Executive Director of the Sierra Club (1952).

The technological and industrial developments of the Cold War era [1945–1991] and a series of surprising events (most notably Donora) fueled a new environmental concern that went beyond saving forests and establishing parks. Carson's bestseller set off a furor with its expose of toxins in consumer products and philosophical claim that controlling nature is both arrogant and morally bankrupt. The Sierra Club prevented the damming of the Grand Canyon and an oil spill at Santa Barbara caused public outrage. The Wilderness Act was passed in 1964 to limit the construction of dams and other structures on important lands and landmarks. During these years the Environmental Protection Agency was founded. The late 1960s and 1970s saw the rise, then, of the modern green movement.

The 1970s saw numerous steps to clean up the environment: the National Environmental Policy Act, the Clean Air Act, the founding of Earth Day, the banning of DDT [a controversial pesticide], the Water Pollution Control Act, and the Endangered Species Act (which the Supreme Court upheld in 1977). Disasters at Love Canal [with the discovery of buried toxic waste] in 1978 and Three Mile Island [the site of a nuclear power plant accident] in 1979 terrified the public with the visible consequences of toxic waste, pollution, and contamination. The 1980s were plagued with oil spills (the [oil tanker] *Exxon Valdez* in 1989, among others), and while there was continued significant backlash from industry against environmental strictures, the various Acts were not overturned.

Environmental Activism

The 1990s saw the offshoot of radical environmentalism in the face of corporate mistreatment of the land—and groups like PETA [People for the Ethical Treatment of Animals], Earth First and ELF [Environmental Life Force] got plenty of media attention. As conservative radio hosts went on tirades about minnows and the spotted owl and the merits of clear cutting,

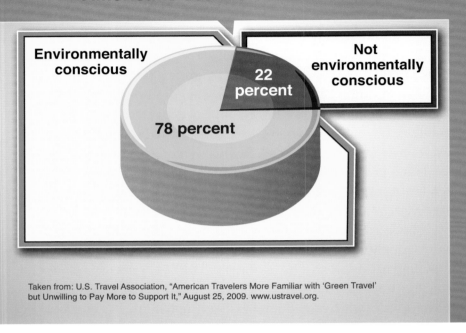

Americans see themselves as . . .

Environmentally conscious

Not environmentally conscious

22 percent

78 percent

Taken from: U.S. Travel Association, "American Travelers More Familiar with 'Green Travel' but Unwilling to Pay More to Support It," August 25, 2009. www.ustravel.org.

passionate young activists famously chained themselves to or took up residence in trees—earning the nickname "treehuggers." These actions gained notoriety, but unfortunately also had the effect of politicizing and emotionally charging key environmental issues. Environmental protection was alternately depicted as being religious, cult-like, anti-society, anti-property ownership and anti-capitalist. Criminal stunts from fringe environmental groups did nothing to dampen the image of environmentalism as extreme. Vegetarianism experienced a popular resurgence with ground-breaking books like *Diet for a New America* ([by John] Robbins) but it also became the brunt of many a late-night comedian's routine. The concept of climate change was ridiculed by many as an overreaction from misguided "environmentalist wackos."

Sobering international events, catastrophic weather, visible climate change, 9/11 [the date in 2001 when terrorists hijacked and crashed American planes] and war, gas shortages and scientific consensus legitimized environmental concerns during the early years of the new century. [Former vice president] Al Gore's blockbuster film *An Inconvenient Truth* seared the climate crisis into the popular consciousness. Suddenly, the problems were obvious everywhere you looked: our food was chemically treated and genetically modified, our water was contaminated with toxic chemicals, our resources were running out, our wasteful habits were filling landfills, New Orleans was virtually destroyed [after Hurricane Katrina of 2005], and gas prices were soaring— to name but a few key issues that have spurred millions to "go green."

This [viewpoint] merely reviews the environmental movement as it relates to the United States. Consider: American leaders have yet to sign the Kyoto Protocol [an international treaty aimed at reducing greenhouse gas emissions] or earmark serious funding to green-collar jobs and sustainable technologies and energy. But American citizens have taken it upon themselves [to] join a global movement, to learn more despite the gridlock in Washington [D.C.]; to conserve, to drive the development of eco-friendly consumption, to buy hybrids or use mass transit, even to telecommute. More and more people now recycle, compost, "go organic," grow gardens and understand the connection between saving money, improving health and helping the environment. More people are interested in technology and efficient living than ever before. And more and more people are becoming curious about the natural world in all its majesty and strangeness.

The great opportunity is that every individual can be a part of the green revolution in some way. Everyone can learn and take a positive step in a greener direction. No one's perfect, but together we can solve the problems we face. Welcome to the "new" green movement.

TWO

Going Green Can Stop Global Warming

Bill McKibben

> Bill McKibben is a journalist, a teacher, and the author of *The End of Nature*. His work focuses on climate change and sustainability. In the following viewpoint McKibben discusses the worldwide problem of global warming and describes how green energy and energy conservation can stop global warming. He warns of the problem's effects on glaciers, agricultural output, the world's poor communities, and biodiversity. Beyond energy independence at the national level, McKibben says that individuals can help by revising household lighting, updating appliances, and eating foods from local farmers.

A t any given moment we face as a society an enormous number of problems: there's the mortgage crisis, the health care crisis, the endless war in Iraq, and on and on. Maybe we'll solve some of them, and doubtless new ones will spring up to take their places. But there's only one thing we're doing that will be easily visible from the moon. That something is global warming. Quite literally it's the biggest problem humans have ever faced, and while there are ways to at least start to deal with it, all of them rest on acknowledging just how large the challenge really is.

Bill McKibben, "First, Step Up," *Yes!* Spring 2008. Reproduced by permission of the publisher and the author.

The Global Warming Problem

What exactly do I mean by large? Last fall [2007] the scientists who study sea ice in the Arctic reported that it was melting even faster than they'd predicted. We blew by the old record for ice loss in mid-August, and by the time the long polar night finally descended, the fabled Northwest Passage was open for navigation for the first time in recorded history. That is to say, from outer space the Earth already looks very different: less white, more blue.

What do I mean by large? On the glaciers of Greenland, 10 percent more ice melted last summer than any year for which we have records. This is bad news because, unlike sea ice, Greenland's vast frozen mass sits above rock, and when it melts, the oceans rise—potentially a lot. James Hansen, America's foremost climatologist, testified in court last year that we might see sea level increase as much as six meters—nearly 20 feet—in the course of this century. With that, the view from space looks very different indeed (not to mention the view from the office buildings of any coastal city on earth).

What do I mean by large? Already higher heat is causing drought in arid areas the world over. In Australia things have gotten so bad that agricultural output is falling fast in the continent's biggest river basin, and the nation's prime minister [Kevin Rudd] is urging his people to pray for rain. Aussie native Rupert Murdoch is so rattled he's announced plans to make his NewsCorp empire (think Fox News) carbon neutral. Australian voters ousted their old government last fall, largely because of concerns over climate.

What do I mean by large? If we'd tried we couldn't have figured out a more thorough way to make life miserable for the world's poor, who now must deal with the loss of the one thing they could always take for granted—the planet's basic physical stability. We've never figured out as efficient a method for obliterating other species. We've never figured out another way to so fully degrade the future for everyone who comes after us.

Or rather, we have figured out one other change that rises to this scale. That change is called all-out thermo-nuclear war, and so far, at least, we've decided not to have one. But we haven't called off global warming. Just the opposite: in the 20 years that we've known about this problem, we've steadily burned more coal and gas and oil, and hence steadily poured more carbon dioxide [CO_2] into the atmosphere. Instead of a few huge explosions, we've got billions of little ones every minute, as pistons fire inside engines and boilers burn coal. . . .

The Solution to Global Warming

We need to conserve energy. That's the cheapest way to reduce carbon. Screw in the energy-saving lightbulbs, but that's just the start. You have to blow in the new insulation—blow it in so thick that you can heat your home with a birthday candle. You have to plug in the new appliances—not the flat-screen TV, which uses way more power than the old set, but the new water-saving front-loading washer. And once you've got it plugged in, turn the dial so that you're using cold water. The dryer? You don't need a dryer—that's the sun's job.

We need to generate the power we use cleanly. Wind is the fastest growing source of electricity generation around the world—but it needs to grow much faster still. Solar panels are increasingly common—especially in Japan and Germany, which are richer in political will than they are in sunshine. Much of the technology is now available; we need innovation in financing and subsidizing more than we do in generating technology.

We need to change our habits—really, we need to change our sense of what we want from the world. Do we want enormous homes and enormous cars, all to ourselves? If we do, then we can't deal with global warming. Do we want to keep eating food that travels 1,500 miles to reach our lips? Or can we take the bus or ride a bike to the farmers' market? Does that sound romantic to you? Farmers' markets are the fastest-growing part or the American food economy; their heaviest users may be urban-dwelling immigrants, recently enough arrived from the rest of the world that they can remember what actual food tastes

Wind is the fastest-growing source of electricity around the world, and increasing its use will lower carbon emissions from other sources.

like. Which leads to the next necessity: We need to stop insisting that we've figured out the best way on Earth to live. For one thing, if it's wrecking the Earth then it's probably not all that great. But even by measures of life satisfaction and happiness, the Europeans have us beat—and they manage it on half the energy use per capita. We need to be pointing the Indians and the Chinese hard in the direction of London, not Los Angeles; Barcelona, not Boston. . . .

Americans' Perceptions of the U.S. Role in Global Warming Reduction, 2009

What grade would you give the U.S. government for its efforts to reduce global warming?

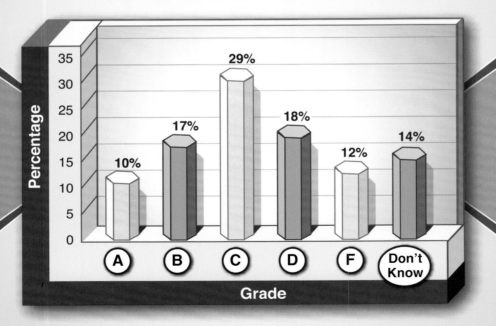

Taken from: Public Agenda, "2009 Energy Learning Curve Report," August 25, 2009. www.publicagenda.org.

Working Together to Go Green

Here's the political reality check, just as sobering as the data about sea ice and drought: China last year passed the United States as the biggest emitter of carbon on Earth. Now, that doesn't mean the Chinese are as much to blame as we are—per capita, we pour four times more CO_2 into the atmosphere. And we've been doing it for a hundred years, which means it will be decades before they match us as a source of the problem. But they—and the Indians, and the rest of the developing world behind them—are growing so fast that there's no way to head off this crisis without their participation. And yet they don't want to participate, because they're using all that cheap coal not to pimp out an already lavish lifestyle, but to pull people straight out of deep poverty.

Which means that if we want them not to burn their coal, we're going to need to help them—we're going to need to supply the windmills, efficient boilers, and so on that let them build decent lives without building coal-fired power plants.

Which means, in turn, we're going to need to be generous, on a scale that passes even the Marshall Plan that helped re-build post–World War II Europe. And it's not clear if we're capable of that any more—so far our politicians have preferred to scapegoat China, not come to its aid.

I said at the start that this was not just another problem on a list of problems. It's a whole new lens through which we look at the world. When we peer through it, foreign policy looks entirely different: the threats to our security can be met only by shipping China technology, not by shipping missiles to China's enemies.

When we peer through the climate lens, our economic life looks completely changed: we need to forget the endless expansion now adding to the cloud of carbon and concentrate on the kind of durability that will let us last out the troubles headed our way.

Our individual lives look very different through these glasses too. Less individual, for one thing. The kind of extreme independence that derived from cheap fossil fuel—the fact that we need our neighbors for nothing at all—can't last. Either we build real community, of the kind that lets us embrace mass transit and local food and co-housing and you name it, or we will go down clinging to the wreckage of our privatized society.

Which leaves us with the one piece of undeniably good news: we were built for community. Everything we know about human beings, from the state of our immune systems to the state of our psyches, testifies to our desire for real connection of just the kind that an advanced consumer society makes so difficult. We need that kind of community to slow down the environmental changes coming at us, and we need that kind of community to survive the changes we can't prevent. And we need that kind of community because it's what makes us fully human.

This is our final exam, and so far we're failing. But we don't have to put our pencils down quite yet. We'll see.

THREE

Going Green Cannot Stop Global Warming

Geoffrey Pike

Geoffrey Pike is a frequent contributor to the news and commentary Web site LewRockwell.com. In the following viewpoint Pike argues that green activism has no effect on global warming or the environment. Pike argues specifically against the need for conservation, recycling, and fuel-efficient vehicles. He concludes that the green environmental movement wastes time, energy, and resources while providing no value to society.

There is a movie called *Idiocracy* in which two average people partake in a hibernation project and end up 500 years in the future. To their surprise, the people in society have turned into complete idiots. Sometimes I feel like this is the world I am living in, especially lately with Earth Day.

The whole "green" movement is a joke and I am baffled by how many people have been swindled out there. I have nothing against others helping the environment or nature, provided that it is done peacefully, but all of this environmental anguish is out of control. Luckily, the average American is only talking about it and doing small symbolic gestures and is not ready to sacrifice their lifestyle.

Most of the so-called solutions we hear from so-called environmentalists are not really solutions at all. They are ideas that simply make life for human beings more difficult and more expensive, while slowing down human progress. The whole so-called environmental movement is anti-human and anti-freedom. When communism collapsed in the late 80's and early 90's, it was given a bad name association, and rightly so. The communists had to go into hiding and could no longer directly call for communism since their ideas [of common property and organized labor, with the goal of a classless society] had been discredited. The communists decided to become environmentalists and take a new approach to their agenda.

If you'll notice, nearly every single solution offered by the green movement is to impede human progress. It also usually involves using the force of government or at least it is a suggestion that could later lead to government force.

Global Warming Is Not a Problem

The whole global warming debate has to be a hoax. We live in a variable climate that has always varied as long as mankind has walked the earth. If this year is warmer than last year, it means nothing. If this century is warmer than last century, it means nothing. Next week may be warmer or colder than this week. It could go either way because we live in a variable climate. Even the reports that the earth has warmed in the last century can be doubted. Some of the official thermometers have been found to be within a short distance of pavement that attracts heat.

If the earth has actually warmed by a degree in the last century, so what? The century before that may have been 2 degrees warmer. If you ever get a chance to see Greenland, you will find that it is mostly ice. There isn't much green to it. But the people that settled Greenland probably named it that for a reason. Could it have been much warmer there when it was first settled centuries ago?

Even if the earth is warming, it doesn't mean it has anything to do with humans. Most of the scientists that preach man-made global warming get their funding from government. If they didn't preach man-made global warming, then their funding would miraculously disappear. It is amazing how incentives work. If the earth is warming, it might not be such a bad thing, especially for some of the brutal places near the poles. But even if we did want to stop global warming from occurring, we certainly shouldn't turn to government and another FEMA [Federal Emergency Management Agency]-like agency.

Environmental Activism Is Not Necessary

Another green idiocracy issue is that of saving water. The last time I checked, about two-thirds of the earth is covered in water. There is this incredible process where water evaporates and is purified and falls as fresh water from the clouds. It is like a huge filtration system for our planet.

It makes no sense when people talk about saving water. We pay for water when we pay our water bill. The more water you use, the more you pay for it. It is just like any other good that we buy. When you see areas that have a drought and a supply problem with water, that is an automatic indication that the government is interfering. In a normal free market, if there is an increase in demand or a decrease in supply of something, the price rises. This will decrease demand and may help increase the supply if the good can be obtained from another place that has a larger supply.

In areas with droughts, the government control of the water supply is really the only reason for a shortage. If you walk into a grocery store in those areas, there will be plenty of bottled water on the shelves as this operates in a more free market environment.

Then we have recycling. I have nothing against recycling, just government forced recycling. This includes being forced to pay for others to recycle. If it is worth it to recycle a particular material, then the free market will take care of this. If the government forces you to pay for a recycling program, then it is not cost effective. For example, if it costs an average of 5 cents per

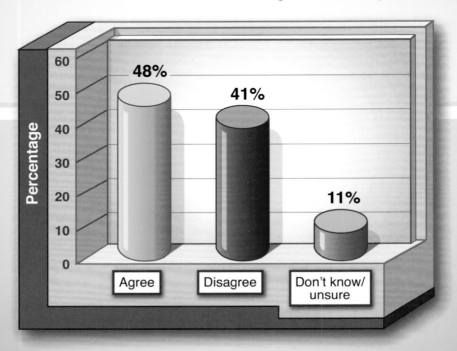

Agree or Disagree: Major sacrifices are required in order to reduce the effects of global warming.

Taken from: Public Agenda, "2009 Energy Learning Curve Report," August 25, 2009. www.publicagenda.org.

can to recycle soda cans and it saves only 4 cents per can in making new ones, then it is not worth it. However, if they could be recycled at a cost of only 3 cents per can to later save 4 cents, then it may be worth it and some company may come in and do it and give you a monetary incentive to participate. But if the government has to subsidize it, then it is a waste of money.

The Power of the Free Market
The same goes for more fuel-efficient vehicles. If the price of gas gets high enough, it will be worth it for people to pay more for

hybrid and other fuel-efficient vehicles. You shouldn't need a government subsidy.

This also applies to ethanol. If using corn to make ethanol for our gasoline were an efficient use of resources, the government would not have to "give" out billions of dollars in subsidies. It actually uses more energy to make ethanol from corn than it produces, but this fact doesn't even matter. If it were really cheap to make ethanol or if ethanol could make your car get 500 miles to the gallon, then people would freely choose to use it out of their own self-interest. But when the government has to force us to pay for it, we can all be certain that it is a waste of resources.

Anti-global warming views are expressed at the climate change forum at the University of California–Los Angeles. Some think the free market will solve global warming.

The ironic thing about the whole environment issue is that the governments of the world are by far the biggest destroyers of it. When you hear about one of those forest fires raging in California, it most likely originated on government land. The best answer to having a good environment is through strong property rights. When individuals are secure in their property, they can confront those that infringe on their property with pollution or anything else, as the justice system would provide a remedy of the situation with possible restitution. And more, when property is owned privately and not through the government, it is much more likely to be taken care of. People will treat their own property with the respect that it deserves, whereas government property will be abused, neglected, and possibly destroyed.

People need to stop being so phony about going green and start thinking with their heads. The green movement today does little, at best, to help the environment and it is a total waste of time and resources.

FOUR

Small Changes Can Make a Difference

Howard Gordon

> Howard Gordon is the executive producer of the Fox tele-
> vision series *24* and a contributor to the *Jewish Journal*. In
> the following viewpoint Gordon discusses the small steps
> that he and his family have taken to go green. Initially a
> skeptic, Gordon slowly accepted that his actions could add
> up to make a difference. And by greening his behaviors,
> Gordon says, others followed his example and started to
> change their own wasteful habits.

All right, I admit it. When it came to believing that I could make a difference in the fight to stop global warming, I was a skeptic. Sure, I drove a Prius, and I dutifully deposited my Fiji bottles in the nearest blue recycling bin. But the truth is, I mostly did these things to make my wife, Cami, feel better. She's been such a true believer for such a long time that I had no real choice in the matter if I wanted to keep the peace at home.

So I humored her passionate activism, I indulged her fears in the dire predictions being offered up daily by scientists and by the media. Not that I didn't believe that our consumer society is on the fast track to destroying the planet—I just didn't think that anything I did was going to derail the inevitable.

On more than one occasion, I slipped and admitted to my wife my true feelings on the subject. That we were hypocrites. Limousine liberals. Driving a Prius might make us feel better about ourselves, but it didn't compensate for all the carbon we were emitting by employing the small army of people who help maintain our not-so-modest home—from gardeners to house cleaners to handymen. These are people who commute from far-away places in cars far less efficient than ours. If we really wanted to reduce our carbon footprint, we should sell our house, move into a high-rise, and take public transportation.

Starting Small

We had this argument at least a dozen times. And each time, my wife held her ground, insisting that doing something was better than doing nothing. She said if everyone did something, it would make a difference.

So I'd grudgingly go back to carrying my own canvas bags to the supermarket, unplugging my cellphone charger, even trading in my Fiji water for a refillable aluminum bottle. Until one day, the light bulb went off over my own head. Literally.

I was replacing an incandescent bulb with a more efficient compact fluorescent bulb [CFB], and when I turned it on to test it, I suddenly realized that the skepticism I'd been carrying with me for all this time had given way to something else. Something that felt a lot like satisfaction. The solution was never going to come all at once; it was a process. By doing these small things, however reluctantly, I'd begun to believe that I really was making a difference. And that was the whole point of doing something, of doing anything that contributed to the solution.

Having taken these few halting, reluctant steps, I found myself looking forward to taking more steps. Carrying the canvas bags to the supermarket stopped feeling like a hassle. I went out of my way to carpool with people I knew were attending school events and business meetings. I had solar panels installed at our house. I even headed up an effort to make more energy efficient the physical production of the television show I produce, *24*, as

Simply screwing in a compact fluorescent lightbulb in lieu of a conventional bulb is but one of many effortless and satisfying ways to go green.

part of News Corp.'s Cool Climate Change initiative. I'd finally joined Cami on what had been, until now, her solo journey.

Small Changes Influence Others

Perhaps most significantly, I realized that our actions, small and large, were starting to change the behavior of the people around us. Because we've been making choices to reduce our carbon

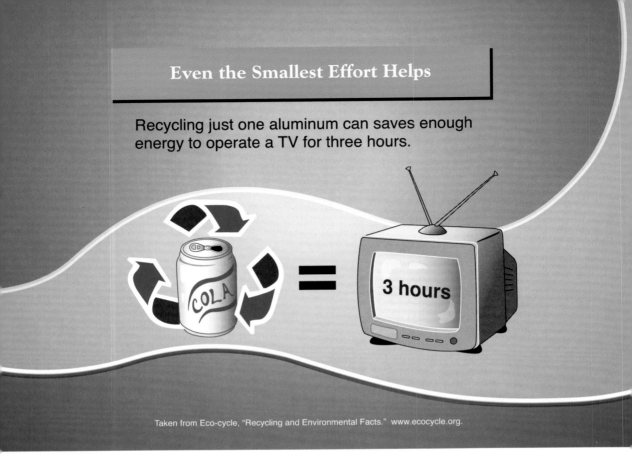

Even the Smallest Effort Helps

Recycling just one aluminum can saves enough energy to operate a TV for three hours.

COLA = 3 hours

Taken from Eco-cycle, "Recycling and Environmental Facts." www.ecocycle.org.

footprint, the people around us are starting to take their own first steps to reduce theirs. Our children are getting pretty good at turning off the lights when they're not in a room, and turning down the heat. Some of our friends have started replacing their incandescent bulbs with CFLs.

Now and again, that familiar skepticism comes back. Bringing my own mug to Starbucks still doesn't seem like much of an answer to the massively rising energy consumption happening in India and China. And I'm waiting for a DWP [Department of Water and Power] audit to find out how much energy those solar panels of mine are really producing. But even if it doesn't turn out to be as much as I'd like, we're still doing better than we would have been doing without them—and not nearly as good as I hope we'll all be doing in the future.

FIVE

Small Changes Do Not Make a Difference

Sarah Fenske

> Sarah Fenske is an award-winning feature columnist and journalist for the *Phoenix New Times*. In the following viewpoint Fenske argues that small changes in lifestyle, behavior, and purchasing decisions will not help to reduce global warming. Fenske describes some of the bigger changes that would have to be made on a much larger scale in order to make an impact on global warming. And she contends that most people will be unwilling to accept the inconveniences and costs of those big changes.

Last year [2007], trees died so I could learn how to live "green."

Doesn't seem quite right, does it? But anybody with a magazine jones like mine undoubtedly triggered a similar herbicide. That's because *Vanity Fair* and *Dwell* and *Elle* and *Shape* and *Wired* have each produced a "green issue" (or three), and now even the local guys, like *Java* and *Phoenix* and *Desert Living*, are joining in. Even though glossy magazines kill an estimated 15 trees per ton of paper, each one is intent on spreading the gospel of just how easy it is to Save the Earth.

Usually, in fact, it boils down to supporting the issue's advertisers: Buy a [low emission Toyota] Prius! Buy an organic cotton T-shirt! Buy vegan nail polish remover!

And then there's *Big Green Purse*. Perhaps I was subconsciously influenced by all those green issues, or maybe I'm just a sucker for trendy books. For whatever reason, I recently spent $17.95 on a 411-page book telling me I could save the world through shopping. Yes, the paper was recycled, but that's still a lot of freakin' pulp to provide such helpful suggestions as "buy a vest or sweatshirt made from recycled soda bottles." (I can't say I was particularly tempted.)

Green Is Big Business

These days, helping the environment is Big Business. It's not just media hype, and not just sweatshirts made from post-consumer Diet Coke packaging. The Phoenix Zoo is going green with a contest for kids to design new recycling bins. High-end restaurants, like Scottsdale's Mosaic, are selling organic wine right next to pricey Italian reds. It's hard to find a new development in the [high-tech business hub Silicon] Valley that isn't being marketed as "sustainable," no matter how iffy the design.

The hype has gotten so bad that David Leibowitz, vice president at the Phoenix advertising firm Moses Anshell, tells me that he actually considered buying a Hummer just to cancel out what he calls the "greener than thou" cabal buying Priuses. (He ultimately settled for a midsize SUV [sport utility vehicle].)

"Right now," Leibowitz says, "Green is unavoidable in a really aggravating way."

But the current ubiquity of eco-trendiness isn't just annoying. It's also dangerous.

Bigger Solutions Are Needed

Everybody wants to believe there's a quick and painless way to make a difference. "Never doubt that a small group of thoughtful, committed citizens can change the world," etc., etc.

California governor Arnold Schwarzenegger announces that the Southern California Edison power company will build the nation's largest solar installation. It will be capable of generating power for 162,000 homes. More big projects like this one are needed, critics say.

No offense to Margaret Mead [twentieth-century cultural anthropologist], but in this case, it's simply not true.

I read *Big Green Purse*. (I had to justify killing those trees, after all.) As I read, I actually made a list of all the suggestions included therein that I'd be willing to try. Pick one day a week, author Diane MacEachern urged, to wear no makeup. That's not so hard, right? She also urged women not to douche (something about the chemicals involved) and to buy fewer cleaning products (again, chemicals). I was starting to feel pretty good about myself. After all, I hadn't bought a new cleaning product in six months, much less shot it into my nether region.

But the more I kept reading, the queasier I became. I began to realize I could do every single thing Diane MacEachern wanted me to do, and it wouldn't make one iota of difference.

That's because our big environmental problems don't come from mascara, or even Clorox. The real problem is our reliance on old coal-burning power plants, big gas-guzzling cars, and suburban McMansions.

You can have as many makeup-free days as you want; if you're living in a five-bedroom house in Buckeye and working in Queen Creek, you're not doing a lick of good. The little stuff simply doesn't matter if the big picture is a wasteful mess.

Here's an example: Diane MacEachern herself casually mentions flying to Tanzania for vacation. Twice. According to the various "carbon footprint" calculators I consulted, those two trips alone created more harmful carbon dioxide emissions than I generated in an entire year—and I'm a dry-clean-only, V-6 engine-driving carnivore!

The more I noodled around with the science behind every green issue's oh-so-easy suggestion, the more I realized this effort can't be about the small stuff.

We can each do our part. We can stop wearing makeup, we can forage for our own locally grown sustainable foods, and we can even limit our wardrobes to undyed wool from free-range alpacas, much as I'd advise against it for aesthetic reasons. But as long as you, or even your neighbor, is regularly flying to Tanzania, or even just driving an Escalade to work, it's not going to have much of an impact.

Sorry.

Bigger Solutions Are Difficult to Implement

There really are things we can do to save the Earth, if that's our cup of tea.

The problem is, we're not doing them. And why should we? We think we're making a difference by buying organic cotton instead of polyester. (Never mind that we could actually do the most good, ecologically speaking, by staying away from the mall, period. Of course that idea doesn't sell advertising, and could well destroy the economy if practiced *en masse* [all together], so don't expect to see it in a green issue near you any time soon.)

That's why I think all this stuff is ultimately so dangerous: There's a real risk that the quick-and-easy ideas pushed by "green" marketers everywhere are only going to numb us to the real solutions—solutions that might, in fact, prove painful.

Leibowitz, the advertising guy, pointed me toward a recent BBMG [Branding and Integrated Marketing] poll, first cited in *Brandweek*. The poll found that while 28 percent of consumers said it was "very important" to buy from companies who do good things for the planet, only 17 percent reported "always" doing so.

Even that number, I'm betting, is inflated. "Always?" Just as suspicious is the 16 percent who reported taking a reusable bag with them while shopping. Just go to Whole Foods some day and watch the line. You may be at the most cheerfully "green" grocery chain around, but you're still not going to see one out of every six shoppers putting their groceries into little cloth bags.

Or take solar panels. Jim Arwood, director of the energy office of the Arizona Department of Commerce, is a big believer in solar power. Solar panels on his roof supply almost half of the energy used by his household. Even better, because the panels connect to the electric grid, the energy produced by those panels is never wasted. It goes back into the system to provide power for other homes, reducing the state's reliance on dirtier forms of energy—and earning Arwood credits from APS [Arizona Public Service Company] in the process.

People Are Reluctant to Change
But here's the rub.

Arwood is one of only 1,642 people in the entire state who've put up panels connecting to the grid. Seven times as many Arizonans voted for [2008 Republican candidate] Fred Thompson *after* he quit the presidential race. Forty-two times as

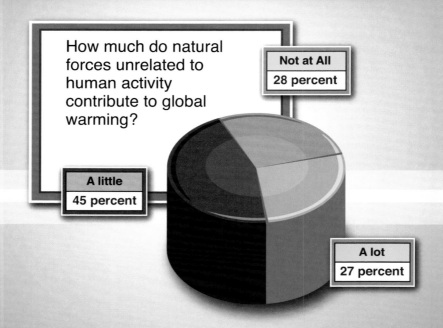

Many Americans Believe Global Warming Is Unrelated to Human Activity

How much do natural forces unrelated to human activity contribute to global warming?

Not at All
28 percent

A little
45 percent

A lot
27 percent

Taken from: Public Agenda, "2009 Energy Learning Curve Report," August 25, 2009. www.publicagenda.org.

many people have outstanding warrants for their arrest in Maricopa County alone.

It's truly ridiculous. We're living in the sunniest state in the Union. We have tax incentives up the ying-yang. Students at Arizona State University's School of Global Management recently concluded that, thanks to those two factors, a medium-size set of panels would pay for itself in approximately 17 years. For an upper-middle-class family, that's not a bad equation.

And yet, for all the green hype flooding my mailbox, hardly anybody is doing it. California last year launched a "Million Solar Roofs" initiative, with the goal of plugging that many homes into the grid.

In Arizona, we'll be lucky to get 100,000.

Jim Arwood knows that he's still in a very small minority when it comes to personal solar generation, but he's optimistic.

He clearly thinks I'm way too cynical about this state's under-utilization of solar. "Thirty years ago, the 'solar industry' was a handful of backyard inventors," he says. "It takes time, but we're making a whole lot of progress."

But the path that progress is taking, I think, illustrates a bigger truth.

We can talk all we want about free enterprise, and individuals taking responsibility. We can read 411-page books designed to make us more green.

But we're not going to convert even a fraction of the state to renewable resources by depending on well-meaning individuals. Just look at how few homes have bothered to finance solar panel systems. If it isn't as easy as flashing a credit card or dropping an empty Coke can into a recycling bin, most of us simply won't do it.

Bigger Solutions Are Expensive

And if it's not leading to a new outfit, even a credit card swipe has proved too difficult for 99 percent of us. Literally. APS has a "Green Choice" program, in which customers can opt to pay a little extra to get power from renewable sources. A spokesman says it costs the average household only about $11 a month. Still, fewer than 1 percent of the utility's customers have opted in.

But here's where it gets interesting. Even though individuals have proved utterly unwilling to do the green thing, we keep saying in polls that we care about the environment. You can't blame the politicians for thinking we really mean it.

So Arizona is about to get frog-marched into going green.

Right now, Arizona utilities are required to generate only 1 percent of their power from renewable resources. By 2025, though, the Arizona Corporation Commission is increasing that requirement to 15 percent. That's huge—and Arwood believes it's already making a difference. He points to the three-square-mile Solana Generating Station proposed for the Gila Bend area. It will rely on new technology to turn solar power into electricity, with a complexity far beyond the simple heat-storing rooftop panels.

In its first year, Solana is expected to generate 20 times more solar power than the entire *state* generates today.

Solana has its drawbacks. Despite its huge size, it's expected to generate enough power for only 70,000 homes, a mere fraction of the state's load. And it won't be cheap. Its energy will be 20 percent more costly than traditional sources. Hey, you said you wanted to save the Earth, right?

But there's an interesting twist in how it all could work. Thanks to the renewable-energy mandates, power in Arizona is likely to get more expensive. And as that happens, individuals will have more incentive to do their part. After all, a rooftop solar panel system will pay for itself a lot more quickly if the cost of electricity is sky high.

Just look at California. Because of heavy demand there, and local environmental pressures that have kept new coal-burning plants from being built there, it has to rely on power from other states. It's not cheap.

But the very expensiveness of power has created an interesting opportunity for private enterprise.

"In California, we're seeing companies putting solar panels on residential homes and maintaining them—and it doesn't cost the homeowner anything up front," Arwood says. In essence, electricity is so precious to our western neighbor that private companies have found it worth their while to harness individual roofs.

The Public Bill for Green Incentives

It could happen here. And with that 15 percent mandate looming for the power companies by 2025, it could come sooner than we think.

As a conservative, I get frustrated when I hear people say that corporations need to subsidize this or that. As if you and I don't ultimately pay for corporate subsidies in higher prices! Same for government programs. If the government is picking up the tab for "solar incentives," ultimately, you and I are picking up the bill.

So it's kind of funny that the poll cited in *Brandweek* concludes that consumers want companies to do more for the environment than they'll do as individuals. Nice try, people. That's not how it works, not ultimately.

We may be opting only for the quick-and-easy solutions today. But if this whole eco-friendly trend goes anywhere, we're all ultimately going to pay the price.

That may well be a good thing. Clean air, clean water, and trees may be worth part of our hard-earned pay. But let's be honest about it.

It's not going to be as easy as wearing organic clothes and cutting back on the lip liner. It will require expense—and hard choices.

I may even have to give up a magazine subscription or two. I'm thinking *Vanity Fair*. After all, if the name of the game is sacrifice, putting the Material Girl on the cover of your green issue is just plain stupid.

SIX

Reducing Purchases Can Make a Difference

Clayton Dach

Clayton Dach is a journalist and frequent contributor to *AdBusters* magazine and Web site. In the following viewpoint Dach discusses the differences between the way his parents and grandparents lived and today's modern way of life. He identifies the need for people to reduce the amount of goods that they purchase and use and, in turn, the waste created from overbuying. Dach suggests that communities can work together, sharing everything from time and knowledge to goods and transportation, to help people reduce such waste.

My dad, like my mom, grew up on a farm among the wheat fields and underwhelming curves of the central Albertan parkland. With a few exceptions like spices and sugar, nearly everything they ate was grown or raised right there, on the farm, with the family's own hands. Sinking one's teeth into a juicy drumstick meant weeks of turning eggs several times a day in an incubator, followed by months of feedings and poo shovelling, followed by a few furious minutes of squawking and thrashing and spurting blood, followed by the plucking and the gutting and the dismembering, followed at last by the actual cooking.

Clayton Dach, "The Simple Life: How to Bring the Land Back to Us," AdBusters.com, September/October 2007. Reproduced by permission.

After all of that, throwing away any part of that chicken would have been nothing short of criminal. (To this day, Dad remains a big fan of the gizzards, while Mom claims to have always loved "sucking the jelly right off of the toe bones.") As for those things that couldn't be grown, edible or otherwise, it was all bought with money from the grain harvest, from selling gallons of cream to the local creamery, or from moonlighting whenever there was slack in the farm work.

No wonder that my mom became a self-styled waste cop. The most rabid recycler I know, she regularly slips other people's garbage into her pockets to be properly sorted once she gets home. The satisfaction that she gets from this doesn't come from some abstract sense of duty to the Earth, but from the thought that all of this valuable stuff—all of this metal, paper, glass, and plastic that so many people sweated so much to produce—will be put to further use.

Her parents' refusal to waste, however, was rooted in memories far more indelible than last summer's hard labour. Three of my grandparents—the three that were born in Canada—came of age during the Great Depression [of the 1930s], which hit the Canadian prairies harder than just about anywhere else. Frugality was burned into their blood. Waste became more than a pile of useless rubbish; it was lost opportunity, something to be eyed with suspicion and disdain.

"We never had a dump to go to," explains my mom, "Scraps and peels and rotten potatoes would go to the pigs, or into the vegetable garden as fertilizer. We reused all of the wooden crates and burlap sacks that our dry goods came in. You could always find a use for paper, lengths of twine, stuff like that. As a last resort, anything that we couldn't use ended up in the burning barrel, and the ashes were fertilizer as well."

It would have taken a pretty heroic resistance for such childhood rituals not to have brainwashed them. If you want evidence of this in my dad, come over one day and take a peek in his garage. Open any drawer or cubby, and you'll find an embarrassment of salvaged wreckage—bolts, washers and rusty nails that pre-date my awkward puberty; evidence of a half-dozen dissected lawnmowers; sparkplugs from a 1988 Toyota Tercel that we never owned—the bulk of which I can't even identify, but for which Dad always seems to be formulating a distant-future plan.

That he has managed to amass so much junk is itself informative. My grandparents' perpetual war against waste was made simpler by the equally frugal people who surrounded them, and who hadn't yet discovered a non-negotiable need for things like disposable milk cartoons, single-use plastic shopping bags, or individually wrapped cucumbers. Our cities, by contrast, actually force these little miracles into the hands of all but the most hyper-vigilant. And whereas granny once had to physically wrangle with every piece of garbage she created, our waste alights from our hands as if on the wings of fairies.

The Best Environmental Action Is to Reduce Purchases

[Environmental author] Adria Vasil knows this reality well. Her new book, *Ecoholic*, sprung from the green advice she dispenses through her regular column in Toronto's *NOW* magazine. She notes that while many of her interrogators write to her for judgements on potential purchases, she's constantly returning to one core principle: "As long as our economy and culture is built around the shop-til-you-drop concept, we'll never really embrace the number one rule of environmentalism, which is to reduce. Our grandparents knew that rule well. Anyone that's lived through a depression does, really."

So what advice does Vasil have to offer those of us striving for granny-like restraint in a decidedly un-granny-like world?

"I always tell people to take a pen and write the word 'reduce' on the back of your hand," she says, "Then go through the rest of your day with that idea in mind. Every time you reach for something, think: Do you really need that bottle of water when you could just drink tap? Do you need to turn that key in your car's ignition when you could bike, walk or bus it?"

This kind of concerted self-discipline may be the only way for us to manufacture a latter-day simulation of the consumption

Current Consumption of Goods and Resources Cannot Be Sustained

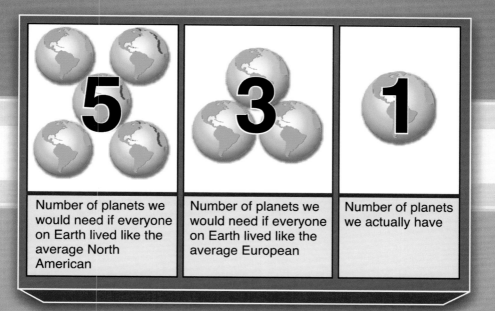

5	3	1
Number of planets we would need if everyone on Earth lived like the average North American	Number of planets we would need if everyone on Earth lived like the average European	Number of planets we actually have

Taken from: Planet Green, "Back to Basics: By the Numbers," 2009. http://planetgreen.discovery.com.

habits of our grandparents, most of whom had neither the money nor the temptation to constantly shop. Alas, the human brain is a stubborn beast, allowing each and every one of us to perform some impressive mental gymnastics when it comes to self-persuasion. In just a few short, strange years, we have managed to assemble, virtually from scratch, a veritable checklist of goods that we all must own to attest to our green credentials. Not so long ago, we suffered through the absurdity of ad campaigns claiming four-wheel-drive SUVs [sport utility vehicles] as the only tools available to us for accessing nature. Now we suffer through ad campaigns claiming hybrid SUVs as the only tools available to us for saving nature. At the intersection between ecological conscience and shopping fever, buying green— not wasting less—has become the new cultural imperative.

"Buying more green stuff will never fix things and rebalance an ecosystem totally out of whack," points out Vasil, "Even if it's an environmentally friendly widget made from biodegradable corn, it still has an ecological footprint and consumed gobs of resources to grow that corn, then process, package and ship it to your door, not to mention the fact that bio-corn plastics come from GMO [genetically modified organism] corn. Yes, it's greener than the non-biodegradable widget on the shelf next to it . . . but the question becomes, did you really need the widget to begin with?"

Managing our waste, then, is about managing our desire—not necessarily an easy thing when you are encircled by come-ons for goods offering status, contentment and power. In our gran and gramps, though, we have proof that it's not a pipedream. Those gallons of cream that my grandma sold would garner my mom, as with her four siblings, no more than a pair of nice Sunday shoes and a dolly at Christmastime, along with a new winter coat in the fall. Rare trips to the nearest food store or a monthly visit from the door-to-door Raleigh salesman may have landed them a chocolate bar or a bag of candy. But these indulgences were infrequent, and even then had strict limitations. . . .

Communities Can Work Together to Reduce Waste

In his new book, *Deep Economy: The Wealth of Communities and the Durable Future*, US environmentalist Bill McKibben argues that we will require a major renegotiation of the idea of community if we are to have any hope of heading off the more disastrous consequences of climate change. "No question we need new technology," he acknowledges via email, "Fossil fuel is at the center of our economic lives, and it will be hard to replace. But more than hydrogen or cellulosic ethanol or anything else, I think we need the technology of community—to learn the lessons of how to do things with each other again."

"Want hard numbers? The average western European uses half as much energy as the average North American—not because they have some different technology but because they have a slightly different approach to the world. Half is a lot—especially considering that their levels of satisfaction with life are higher than ours."

Whether it's sharing space, sharing goods, sharing buying-power, sharing expertise, sharing time or sharing transportation, there are plenty of opportunities to foster our technologies of community, both new and old. Quite aside from merely helping each other out in the fields, my grandparents' generation was instrumental in bringing about what may have been the golden age of the co-op, at least in Canada, where credit unions, co-op insurance, building co-operatives, agricultural pools and consumer co-ops entered a period of astonishing proliferation. Critically, the greatest constituency for these voluntary associations was not ardent intellectuals or politicians nursing an agenda, but rather

In Europe people use only half of the energy Americans use; they also consume less and recycle more.

working rural people who realized that cooperation made wonderful sense for their families and for their larger communities.

So should our goal be to turn back the clock, to reconstitute the organic community and reinvigorate the specific institutions that sprang up to support them?

"More localized economies should help," McKibben offers, "Not in the way that our grandparents lived, precisely, but taking advantage of new ideas too. Visit a modern community-supported agriculture farm—there's all kinds of innovation about compost and green manure and biological pest control, and far less interest in individual self-sufficiency than in community sufficiency." Even in our most impersonal megacities, these new technologies of community are already popping up all around us—from CSAs [Community Supported Agriculture], to car co-ops, to ride-sharing schemes, to district heating networks, to urban community gardens, to farmers' markets. The trick is to seek them out and make a habit out of them. . . .

Lessons from Past Generations

When we outsource every function of our lives, particularly those things that are critical to human life, we also outsource a participatory stake in the future. Without that stake, without a meaningful reason to keep one eye fixed on what's to come, all of the other things that we can do to mitigate our impact on the planet—reducing waste, scaling back our desires, localizing production, sharing resources—will never come to pass.

My grandparents were hardly environmentalists. Along the way, they and their peers were responsible for some pretty stunning missteps. They tended to trust everything that science had to offer, eagerly snatching up DDT [a dangerous pesticide], chemical fertilizers and miracle detergents. They swooned over air travel, the tropical getaway, the 5,000-kilometre pineapple. They started our headlong rush toward the car-centric suburbs, and they made that journey in some very, very hefty automobiles.

"We shouldn't overly romanticize the past," suggests Vasil, "We just have to figure out how to take the best ideas from it, creatively adapt it to the present and make reducing innovative and practical, not just a stodgy drag." Looking to the past, and being innovative at the same time? Everything that I've ever been told about the supremacy of youth has assured me that this is implausible. Yet here I am, in spite of myself, starting to believe it.

The fact is, the 50-year-old promise of youth culture runs nearly parallel to the promise made by modernity itself: the future is brave, prosperous, wholly new; the past is useless, quaint, vaguely embarrassing. This is the promise that billions in developing nations—a sizeable majority of the planet—have been dreaming about for decades. If we're lucky, they'll be able to shake off the fog of that dream faster than we have. If, as a species, we are less than lucky, we may not be so pleased with just how appallingly new the planet can become.

SEVEN

Reusing as Much as Possible Can Make a Difference

Andi McDaniel

Andi McDaniel is a journalist and frequent contributor to *Conscious Choice*, *Ode*, and *Experience Life*. In the following viewpoint McDaniel discusses the "zero waste" movement, which calls for the elimination of all trash. McDaniel outlines ideas for achieving zero waste through better product and packaging designs, more thoughtful purchasing decisions, and a higher rate of reuse for all items. Even some large companies have joined the movement to reduce waste, she says, but more efficient methods and more incentives for reducing and recycling are still needed to increase participation.

Aside from Oscar the Grouch [of Sesame Street], few people would argue that trash is a bad thing. In addition to being stinky, ugly and a pain to lug out to the curb, the detritus of modern life causes problems on a far grander scale. Landfills and incinerators have been linked to a host of human health issues, and as for the environment—you don't have to be an ecologist to know that lingering piles of plastic, metal and toxic goo are bad news all around.

Yet, we continue to throw things away—and how could we not? What else would we do with that annoying cellophane packaging? The to-go boxes? The packing peanuts? The after-dinner scraps that even the dog won't touch?

Part of the solution is as simple as a blue bin. Curbside recycling is still an incredibly effective way to save energy and divert tons of plastics, cans and glass away from landfills. Another answer is composting, which would address more than 60 percent of what ends up in residential dumpsters.

The Zero Waste Movement

But in addition to getting the word out about these tried and true solutions, a new movement is taking a more holistic approach. Rather than focusing solely on what to do with existing waste, the "Zero Waste" movement looks at a product's entire life cycle—and redirects the conversation toward usable options for very step along the way. The ultimate goal is to eliminate waste as a concept entirely—a lofty aspiration indeed. But Zero Wasters say loftiness is part of the point—after all, creating a trash-free world is going to take nothing short of revolution.

The idea behind Zero Waste is simple: basically, nothing with a second use should be thrown away. And if something doesn't have a second use, it shouldn't exist. The Berkeley Ecology Center, a West Coast leader in the Zero Waste movement, puts it this way, "If it can't be reduced, reused, repaired, rebuilt, refurbished, refinished, resold, recycled or composted, then it should be restricted, redesigned or removed from production."

While Zero Waste depends on careful attention to what we do or don't toss in our home trashcans, its ultimate task is to take a bigger view of how waste is handled on an industrial level. According to the Grassroots Recycling Network (GRRN), an international Zero Waste advocacy group, "The goal applies to the whole production and consumption cycle—raw material extraction, product design, production processes, how products are sold and delivered, how consumers choose products and more."

It's one thing to tell consumers to stop throwing banana peels in the trash bin, but quite a larger task to convince industry to adopt Zero Waste. Still, Eric Lombardi, executive director

The idea behind zero waste is that nothing that could be reused should be thrown away. Here a woman recycles a pillowcase by turning it into a bread bag.

of Eco-Cycle, a Zero Waste-oriented non-profit based in Boulder, Colo., says that industry is more amenable to the concept than you'd think. "Waste is money, and industry gets that better than anyone," he explains. In addition to offering various recycling services, Eco-Cycle consults businesses on how to reduce their overall waste. That means spending time peering into the dumpster, where they'll notice trashed items that could have been avoided through smarter purchasing decisions. "We'll agree to pick up those hard-to-recycle items like computers and plastic bags and shoes," he says, "and then what's left? Mostly junk plastics. That's when we talk with the people who do the purchasing to stop buying the things that end up in the dumpster."

Responsible Industry

Of course, industry interest in Zero Waste isn't generally motivated by goodness of heart. One of the principal tenets of the Zero Waste strategy is Extended Producer Responsibility (EPR), which, although new to the United States, is already well established in Europe—in part due to the pressing problem of limited landfill space. In an article for *GreenBiz.com*, Guy Crittenden explains, "True EPR connects producers with the downstream fate (and costs) of their products and packaging . . . [which] drives eco-efficiencies up the value chain, culminating in design for the environment."

The beginnings of an EPR policy in the US are visible in the growing number of landfill bans on toxic products, such as cathode ray tubes, large appliances, tires and electronics. In anticipation of future regulations on waste, some companies are voluntarily devising initiatives for reclaiming their waste, such as Sony's and Apple's takeback recycling programs. Of course, such programs also provide companies with that increasingly precious public relations commodity: green street cred [credibility].

At the very least, Zero Wasters are set on halting incentives to make waste. According to GRRN, "Markets today are heavily influenced by tax subsidies and incentives that favor extraction and wasteful industries." It's mainly for this reason—and not for lack of the appropriate technology—that waste has persisted, even in the wake of increasing environmental awareness. GRRN estimates that we have the existing technology to redirect 90 percent of what currently ends up in landfills.

The Ultimate Recycling

Which begs the question: If we didn't send it to landfills, then where would it go? To recycling centers and municipal compost heaps, partly. But Zero Wasters say we shouldn't just be asking how to get rid of our waste. Just as fungi turn rotting logs into fertile growing material, we should be able to do better than piling up our waste and covering it with dirt. And while it's fun to conceive of wackier and wackier recycled products—corn husks turned into countertops! pencils made from recycled paper money! water bottles morphed into cozy fleece outerwear!—Brenda Platt, of the [Washington] DC-based Institute for Local Self-Reliance (ILSR), stresses the importance of finding the highest use for recyclables, to allay the energy wasted in production. In the case of glass bottles, for example, that would mean refilling them (such as with milk bottles), followed closely by turning them into new bottles, transforming them into art glass, and then maybe making "glassphalt," a material that has been used as an alternative to conventional asphalt since the '70s.

"WELL WE'LL OUT-RECYCLE THEM. WE'LL USE PAPER MADE FROM VEGETABLE PRODUCTS, AND SOY-BASED INK, SO AFTER READING THE MAGAZINE IT COULD THEN BE BOILED, MASHED AND EATEN."

"Well we'll out-recycle them. We'll use paper made from vegetable products and soy-based ink, so after reading the magazine it could then be boiled, mashed and eaten." Cartoon by S. Harris. www.CartoonStock.com.

Such efforts can be facilitated by the existence of local "Resource Recovery Parks" where manufacturing and retail businesses share space, equipment and services, as well as reuse, recycling and composting facilities. In some cases, waste from one business becomes a resource for another business within such parks, creating a closed loop.

There's no doubt that Zero Waste is an idealistic—not near impossible—goal. But whether or not it can be done in every instance, says Eric Lombardi, is really beside the point. "Being on the path to zero is the point," explains Lombardi. "Because once you have established zero as the goal—you being the government, you being a CEO [chief executive officer]—then you have a benchmark against which you can measure your future actions."

Perhaps one of those future actions will be recycling your trashcan.

EIGHT

Recycling Makes Sense

Tom Zeller Jr.

> Tom Zeller Jr. is the editor at large for *National Geographic* magazine. In the following viewpoint Zeller discusses the benefits of recycling and the need for businesses and individuals to share the responsibility of recycling as much as possible. Zeller draws attention not only to the use and disposal of a product, but also to its creation—and the depletion of resources and the pollution linked to that process. He also spotlights Europe as the leader in cooperative recycling of packaging materials.

D oes it make sense to recycle?

The short answer is: Yes.

True, some critics wonder whether mandatory programs are a net benefit, since they can require more trucks consuming energy and belching carbon dioxide into the atmosphere.

"You don't want a large truck carrying around just a few bottles," concedes Matthew Hale, director of EPA's [the Environmental Protection Agency's] Office of Solid Waste. But, he notes, most cities are getting better at reducing the environmental costs of recycling. (They're also working to reduce the economic costs. Many recycling programs still cost more to run than they bring in when they sell the recyclable materials back to manufacturers.)

Consider the true cost of a product over its entire life—from harvesting the raw materials to creating, consuming, and disposing of it—and the scale tips dramatically in recycling's favor. Every shrink-wrapped toy or tool or medical device we buy bears the stamp of its energy-intensive history: mountains of ore that have been mined (bauxite, say, for aluminum cans), coal plants and oil refineries, railcars, assembly lines. A product's true cost includes greenhouse gases emitted in its creation as well as use, and pollutants that cause acid rain, smog, and fouled waterways.

Recycling Works

Recycling—substituting scrap for virgin materials—not only conserves natural resources and reduces the amount of waste that must be burned or buried, it also reduces pollution and the

The Benefits of Recycling

This process reduces carbon emissions equal to those of **33 million** cars.

Eighty-three million tons of material are recycled in the United States each year.

demand for energy. "You get tremendous Btu [British thermal units, the amount of heat needed to raise one pound of water one degree Fahrenheit] savings," Hale says.

In an international study published last year [2007] by the Waste & Resources Action Programme, a British group, researchers compared more than 180 municipal waste management systems. Recycling proved better for the environment than burying or burning waste in 83 percent of the cases.

It makes sense to reuse products, of course, and to reduce consumption altogether, as well as to improve initial product design. But given the rising mounds of waste worldwide, it also makes sense to recycle. . . .

Whether or not a particular material is recycled depends on a number of factors, but the most fundamental question is this: Is there a market for it? Markets for some materials, like car batteries, are highly developed and efficient—not least because strict regulations govern their disposal—and a mature recycling infrastructure has grown up as a result. About 90 percent of all lead-acid batteries are recycled, according to the EPA. Steel recycling, too, has been around for decades, while formalized recycling of yard trimmings has not. Despite the explosive growth of plastics—particularly for use in beverage containers—that industry has been slow to develop recycling infrastructure, with most plastic still going to incinerators or landfills.

The Role of Packaging Debris

Higher hygiene standards, smaller households, intense brand marketing, and the rise of ready-made meals have all contributed to an increase in packaging waste, but international trade may be the biggest factor.

Even simple items like bottles of water now routinely crisscross the globe, meaning that thirst for a few swallows of "product" can generate not just plastic bottles, but also a large amount of other packaging debris—from wrapping film to bin liners to shipping crates.

So far, Europe has led the world in recycling packaging materials—principally through the Packaging and Packaging

In Germany yellow bags of "package waste" wait to be picked up for recycling.

Waste Directive of 1994. The EU [European Union] directive calls for manufacturers, retailers, and others in the product chain to share the recycling burden.

With the exception of hazardous wastes, the United States has been slower to embrace the concept of "extended producer responsibility," as the idea is known, according to Bill Sheehan, director of the Product Policy Institute, a nonprofit research organization in Athens, Georgia. Some municipalities, however, are starting to demand that businesses help cover the costs of recycling.

"Otherwise," Sheehan says, we are "just stimulating the production of more stuff."

NINE

Recycling Does Not Make Sense

Jim Fedako

Jim Fedako is a journalist and frequent contributor to *Mises Daily*. In the following viewpoint Fedako outlines the reasons why recycling is inefficient, costly, and wasteful. He argues that there is no real benefit to recycling and objects to the mandatory recycling programs that exist in many communities. Because supply and demand do not support such programs, Fedako asserts, the time and money tied up in them should be redirected to enable more efficient methods of conservation.

This fall [2005], school kids across the country will again be taught a chief doctrine in the civic religion: recycle, not only because you fear the police but also because you love the planet. They come home well prepared to be the enforcers of the creed against parents who might inadvertently drop a foil ball into the glass bin or overlook a plastic wrapper in the aluminum bin.

Oh, I used to believe in recycling, and I still believe in the other two R's: reducing and reusing. However, recycling is a waste of time, money, and ever-scarce resources. What [libertarian journalist] John Tierney wrote in the *New York Times* nearly 10 years ago is still true: "Recycling may be the most wasteful activity in modern America."

Jim Fedako, "Recycling: What a Waste!" *Mises Daily*, September 22, 2005. Reproduced by permission.

Reducing and reusing make sense. With no investment in resources, I can place the plastic grocery bag in the bathroom garbage can and save a penny or so for some more-pressing need. Reducing and reusing are free market activities that are profitable investments of time and labor.

Any astute entrepreneur will see the benefit of conserving factors of production. Today, builders construct houses using less wood than similar houses built just 20 years ago. In addition, these houses are built sturdier; for the most part anyway.

The Green's [the Green Movement's] love for trees did not reduce the amount of wood used in construction; the reduction was simply a reaction to the increasing cost for wood products. Using less wood makes financial sense, and any entrepreneur worth his profit will change his recipe to conserve wood through better design or by substituting less dear materials for wood products.

Recycling Is Inefficient and Costly

A recent *Mises* [*Daily*] article, "Ethanol and the Calculation Issue," noted the inability to calculate the true cost of producing Ethanol [an alternative fuel]. No one can calculate the cost of all the factors of production in the direction from the highest order labor and land down to the lowest order Ethanol at the pump. Certainly the Chicago School, Keynesians [who advocate a mixed economy, including private and public, governmental involvement], etc., will give the calculation the old college try, to no avail of course. Absent government supports, the price of Ethanol at the pump reveals the most accurate economic cost of producing that fuel.

The same applies to recycling. What is the true cost of all the factors involved in the recycling process? I do not have a clue. Though using Misesian logic [referencing economist Ludwig von Mises, who promoted individual and economic freedom], I know that the cost of recycling exceeds its benefit. This is the simple result of the observation that recycling does not return a financial profit.

I used to recycle; it paid. As a child living in the Pittsburgh area, I would collect and clean used glass containers. After collecting a

Disposal of Trash in the United States

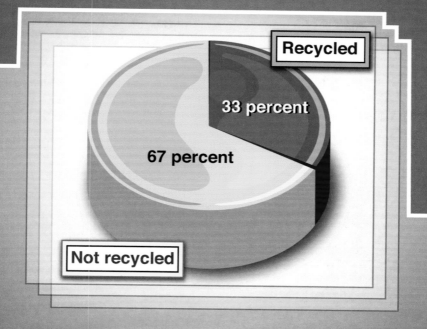

Recycled

33 percent

67 percent

Not recycled

Taken from: U.S. Environmental Protection Agency, "Municipal Solid Waste Generation, Recycling, and Disposal in the United States: Facts and Figures for 2008," November 2009. www.epa.gov.

sufficient amount of glass, my father would drive the three or so miles to the local glass factory where the owner gladly exchanged cleaned waste glass for dollars. In this instance, I was an entrepreneur investing factors of production in order to turn dirty waste glass into capital. The value of the exchange exceeded my preference for time, hard work, and my parents' soap, water, and auto fuel. (Of course all of my exchanges against my parents' resources were high on my preference list, but that is another issue altogether). In this activity, I was not recycling in the standard use of the term. I was producing factors of production —cleaned glass—for a profit.

So, what is wrong with recycling? The answer is simple; it does not pay. In addition, since it does not pay, it is an inefficient use of the time, money, and scarce resources. As Mises would have argued: let prices be your guide. Prices are essential to evaluate actions *ex post* [after the fact]. If the accounting of a near past event reveals a financial loss, the activity was a waste of both the entrepreneur's and society's scarce resources.

That said, I am supposed to believe that I need to invest resources into cleaning and sorting all sorts of recyclable materials for no compensation; an activity that many considered economically efficient. In addition, in some local communities, residents have to pay extra so that a waste company will recycle their paper, plastic, and glass as the recycling bins come with a per-month fee.

In other areas, such as my township, the garbage company profits at the mercy of the political class. The trustees in my township specified that in order to win the waste removal contract, the winning company had to provide recycling bins. Further, they have to send special trucks around to empty those neatly packed bins and deliver the bins' contents to companies that have no pressing need for these unraw materials. The recycling bins are ostensibly free, but in reality, their cost is bundled into my monthly waste removal bill.

There Is No Demand for Recyclable Material

Since there is no market for recyclable materials, at least no market price sufficient to return my investment in soap and water, not to mention time and labor, I conclude that there is no pressing need for recycling.

Ok, but what about the lack of landfills nationwide? If landfills were truly in short supply, then the cost of dumping waste would quickly rise. I would then see the financial benefit to reducing my waste volume. And since the recycling bin does not count toward waste volume, the more in the recycling bin, the less in the increasingly expensive garbage cans. Prices drive entrepreneurial calculations and, hence, human action. Recycling is no different.

Come on now, there cannot be any benefit to even the neoclassical society [with an economic focus on supply and demand] if you actually have to pay someone to remove recyclables.

Since recycling does not turn a profit, it is more efficient to utilize the scarce resources devoted to recycling activities in other modes of production. Instead of wasting resources on recycling, it would be more prudent to invest that money so that entrepreneurs can create new recipes to conserve scarce materials in the production process.

Human action guides resources toward the activities that meet the most pressing needs. This movement of resources means that those activities that do not meet pressing needs are relatively expensive. Why? Those activities have to bid for factors of production along with the profitable activities—activities that are meeting the most pressing needs. The profitable activities will drive the cost of those scarce factors upward leading to financial ruin for those activities that do not satisfy the most pressing needs. Forced recycling is such a failed activity.

Critics of recycling argue that the process is unprofitable and that America has plenty of big landfills to accommodate the country's waste.

The concept of diminishing recyclable resources is fraught with errors. Glass headed to the landfills will sit quietly awaiting someone to desire its value. The glass is not going anywhere, and should glass become as dear as gold—or even slightly less dear, you can bet that entrepreneurs will begin mining landfills for all those junked glass bottles.

The only caveat to this train of thought is what [twentieth-century economist Murray Newton] Rothbard wrote about when he discussed psychic profit: the perceived benefit one receives from performing an action, even if that action leads to an economic loss.

Recycling Should Be Voluntary, Not Forced

Who reaps the real psychic reward from recycling? The statist do-gooder and the obsessed conservationist. Since recycling is now a statist goal, the do-gooders and greens force the cost of recycling on the unsuspecting masses by selling recycling as a pseudo-spiritual activity. In addition to these beneficiaries, there are those who have not considered the full costs of recycling, but their psychic benefit is more ephemeral than real. The other winners are the companies that do the collecting and process the materials, an industry sustained by mandates at the local level.

If recycling at a financial loss leads you to greater psychic profit, then recycle, recycle, recycle. Let your personal preferences guide your actions, but do not force your preference schedule on others who have a different preference rank for their own actions. And, do not delude yourself into thinking that you are economizing anything; you are simply increasing your psychic profit at the expense of a more rational investment. But, hey, your actions are your business; just don't use government to force your preferences on my lifestyle.

Oh, and do not tell my children half the recycling story.

TEN

Choosing Local Food Is Better for the Environment

Jeffrey Hollender

Jeffrey Hollender is the president of Seventh Generation, a brand of green cleaning supplies and paper products, and author of several books, including *What Matters Most* and *Naturally Clean*. In the following viewpoint Hollender describes his experiences with choosing to eat only food grown within one hundred miles of his home. He outlines the benefits and challenges of eating only local food and concludes that benefits can be achieved even with a diet that includes only a portion of local food. In the long run, Hollender says, local foods must be more easily accessible and less costly so that everyone can take advantage of the benefits and take some stress off the environment in return.

Here in Vermont there is a focus on the "localvore" movement, or the practice of eating foods produced much closer to where we live than the trucked- and flown-in food that a majority of Americans buy today. As a way to get people thinking about the idea, quite a few Vermont communities have been holding something called the 100-Mile Challenge, an event in which participants try to eat only things that are grown or raised within 100 miles of their kitchens. It sounded like an interesting experiment. So I gave it a taste drive.

Jeffrey Hollender, "The Localvore Movement," SeventhGeneration.com. Reproduced by permission.

Why Eat Local?

Why play with our food like this? Because eating locally-produced foods is a relatively simple act that provides a bounty of benefits. Most of the food we eat travels between 1,500 and 2,500 miles to get to our plates. When we eat meats and vegetables grown near our homes, we lessen or eliminate the impacts created by those miles, and that helps the world in these crucial ways:

- It protects the environment. Food that travels a long distance uses more fossil fuels, which contribute to pollution, climate change, and other woes. And local food is more likely to come from smaller family farms that generally use more sustainable practices than factory farms.
- It protects our health. Locally-produced food is a lot fresher so it contains more nutrients. It also tastes better because most local farmers grow their crops and raise their livestock for flavor, not for easy processing and shipping. Instead of tomatoes bred to survive a month in a shipping container, we're likely to get heirloom varieties bursting with juice and taste.
- It protects and strengthens our local economies. When we buy locally-produced foods, we support local businesses and keep our dollars circulating in the community. In Vermont, for example, if we could replace just 10% of the foods we eat with local products, we'd create over 3,600 jobs, and add $376 million to the local economy.

Those are some pretty impressive advantages. There's another one, too: When we eat locally, we gain an understanding of where our food comes from. I think that's hugely important because food is fundamental to our lives and yet we know very little about it except that when we need more, we make a trip to the supermarket. For the most part, we have no idea what's involved in filling a salt or pepper shaker. Or making an omelet. Or squeezing a fresh glass of juice. We take all of these things for granted. This kind of unintentional ignorance helps maintain the status quo of our nation's unhealthy industrial food chain and that's not a good thing. When we know where our food comes from and who raised or grew it for us, we know more about both what we're eating and the kind of world it came from. And that means we know more about how to fix both.

The Challenge of Eating Locally

Our present food system doesn't encourage local eating. It doesn't promote family farms or heirloom produce or artisanal cheeses. Based as it is on large-scale factory farming and an ideology that says cheaper is better, the way we've come to eat today doesn't necessarily make the 100-Mile Challenge an easy one. We have to shop a little harder to find local substitutes for the things we

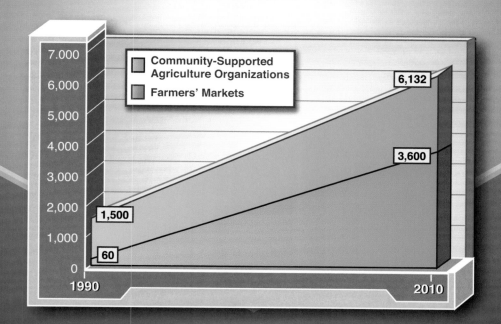

Local Food is Becoming More Readily Available

The numbers of famers' markets and community-supported agricultural organizations in the United States have increased significantly since 1990.

Community-Supported Agriculture Organizations

Farmers' Markets

6,132

3,600

1,500

60

7.000
6,000
5,000
4,000
3,000
2,000
1,000
0

1990   2010

Taken from: U.S. Department of Agriculture, Agricultural Marketing Service, "Farmers' Markets and Local Food Marketing," August 4, 2009. www.ams.usda.gov.

want to eat. We have to get creative when it comes to planning menus. We have to learn to do without in the cases of certain foods and we may have to eat more of other things depending on what's available. It is, in fact, quite challenging indeed.

The good news is that in most parts of the country, it's quite possible to live, at least temporarily, outside the corporate food chain. Here in Vermont, we are especially blessed. In spite of some difficult modern times, we have a decent number of family farms, and many of them are diversifying into organics and value-added products in order to survive.

So we lucky Vermonters can fairly easily find local wine and local beer (though made from imported grains), virtually every dairy product imaginable, including great local cheeses; plenty of locally-baked breads (though, again, the grains they contain are usually from elsewhere); meats that range from beef to bison to chicken and even emu; just about every fresh veggie imaginable (at least during summer); and a great variety of fresh fruits that come and go with their respective seasons.

In fact, it was amazing to me just how bountiful a meal it's possible to create from foods harvested within 100 miles of our home. Using these and other ingredients, we were able on two special occasions to enjoy terrific meals that used only locally-produced ingredients. The first was a meeting between the [green products company] Seventh Generation marketing team and the folks from *Treehugger.com* [a media outlet that focuses on sustainability]. With about 14 people around the table, we dipped our toe in the localvore waters. Next time around, we had about 50 friends who were in town to attend the BALLE [Business Alliance for Local Living Economies] conference. These meals were not the equal of the meals we usually eat. They were better, and thanks to a local agricultural economy that already understands the value of local foods, they didn't require too much extra effort to assemble.

Being Selective About Local Food

Of course, you've probably already read between the lines here and found a bunch of qualifiers in my family's 100-mile experiment.

A farmer readies his locally grown produce for sale at a farmers' market in Vermont. The trend toward using locally produced foods is increasing.

For one, we didn't spend a whole month or even a week eating locally. Our experience consisted of a couple of meals that we undertook as the opportunities presented themselves. Even so, I'd estimate that on a daily basis, we average between 25% to 50% local ingredients. There are some things I am unwilling to give up, including coffee and tea. I think it's perfectly okay to have a few not-from-here things in your pantry as long as you choose them carefully and generally try to stock as locally as possible.

In Vermont and in most parts of North America, eating locally in July is an entirely different proposition from eating locally in January, at which time your choice is roughly between tree bark and whatever dead grass is still poking through the snow. Okay, so it's not quite that bad.

We can stock up and pickle and preserve all kinds of things when they're in season, but we're still going to need some outside culinary help in the colder months if we want a diet with any variety.

And of course, the success each of us has in eating locally depends on what our locality is like. Here in Vermont, it's relatively easy because we haven't yet paved over all our agricultural lands and still have farmers using them. We benefit from a strong local-is-better ethic that has helped many family farms, organic growers, and other producers keep going. Ours is a state tailor-made for the 100-Mile Challenge because its citizens are already doing a lot of the needed work. It might not be as easy in, say, Houston or Phoenix.

Eating Local Food as a Lifestyle

It's also not as easy to eat local if it's a luxury you can't afford. Mass-marketed food is cheaper than the local kind, often by a long shot. This is understandable in the short term but unacceptable in the long run. It's not okay that only those who are well off can afford to eat food that's better for their families and the planet. We need to work to make healthy, organic, local food affordable to all. Some of that will come from ending the hidden subsidies and externalized costs that conspire to make long-distance factory food less expensive. But those who can currently afford the alternative can also move the process along by buying local when and wherever possible. This builds local markets, encourages more local production, and eventually lowers prices as local foods become increasingly plentiful and less "niche market."

For that and many other reasons, we should all try to eat as locally as we can whenever possible. We should all take our own

100-Mile Challenges and work to make this kind of lifestyle the rule rather than the exception. For my part, I need to do more than a meal now and again. And it's something I'm working on. Now that I've taken the first few footsteps on that road, I have a better understanding how it can be done and a better appreciation of the benefits it brings. But Rome wasn't built in a day and neither will a locally-based national food economy. It's something each of us can only do one day and one meal at a time. What's important is not that we all become perfect eaters overnight, but that we're always working toward the goal and toward a harvest of hope we can all share together some day soon.

ELEVEN

Choosing Local Food Is Not Always Better for the Environment

Roberta Kwok

Roberta Kwok is a journalist whose work focuses on science topics. In the following viewpoint Kwok examines the environmental impact of food grown and sold within a hundred-mile radius and food that is imported from long-distance sources. Kwok explains that local food sometimes has a larger carbon footprint than imported food, meaning that local food is not always a better environmental choice. Furthermore, she suggests that consumers should consider criteria beyond carbon emissions, such as water quality impact and geopolitical factors, when making decisions about food sources.

When I arrive at San Francisco's Ferry Plaza Farmers Market on a gray Saturday morning, I do my best to ignore the food. It's not easy. There are mandarin oranges, fresh eggs, piles of perky greens and samples of everything from goat cheese to dried kiwi. But I'm not here to eat; I'm here to hunt for numbers.

A few weeks earlier, I noticed a page on the market's Web site that asks, "How Far Does Food Travel to Get to Your Plate?" Too far, it concludes. According to a 2001 study by the Leopold Center for Sustainable Agriculture, the average apple travels

1,555 miles to a Chicago terminal market where wholesalers sell produce to grocery stores. A San Francisco Farmers Market apple, on the other hand, only travels about 105 miles to the Ferry Plaza market building.

The Web site relies on the concept of "food miles," or the distance that food travels from farm to consumer. A new breed of eaters has embraced the local, low-food-mile diet. The Bay Area–based Locavores group, for instance, vows to eat food produced within 100 miles of San Francisco. In a nod to the movement's growing popularity, the word "locavore" nabbed the title of 2007 Word of the Year from the *New Oxford American Dictionary*, and *Food and Wine* magazine offers tips to befuddled cooks on "How to Eat Like a Locavore." Campaigns such as "Local Food Is Miles Better" (run by the trade magazine *Farmers Weekly* in the United Kingdom) have called on supermarkets to crack down on excessive food miles by labeling and promoting

The Ferry Plaza's Farmers' Market in San Francisco offers produce that has been grown within one hundred miles of the city. Consumers of local produce are called "locavores."

locally produced items. The corporate world has jumped on board as well: Google's Cafe 150 stocks its pantry with ingredients gathered from within a 150-mile radius.

Is Local Better?

While locavores list numerous reasons for eating local—including freshness, taste and boosting regional economies—one primary argument is protection of the environment. Long-distance food transport sucks up more fossil fuels, says the Farmers Market Web site, and unleashes more carbon dioxide onto our planet.

That does sound dire. But what if conventional distributors make up for the long journeys by driving big trucks packed with produce? Let's say a distributor travels 1,000 miles and carries 1,000 apples to market, while 10 local farmers each drive a pickup 100 miles and carry 100 apples each. The local farmers log fewer food miles but cover the same total distance—and use a comparable amount of fossil fuels—for the same amount of food.

Vehicle types and packing likely make a difference, says Richard Pirog, associate director of the Leopold Center for Sustainable Agriculture, and lead author of the food miles study. "I bet you dollars to doughnuts that at your San Francisco Farmers Market, the farmers don't pull up in semi-trailers," he says.

He's right. After surveying 19 farmers on my Saturday visit, I found that most of them drove Ford, Isuzu or Chevrolet trucks, packing anywhere between 200 and 2,000 pounds of goods. While some were hanging onto late '90s models, one proudly sported a new fuel-efficient Dodge Sprinter. They'd trucked their wares an average of 117 miles, with farms ranging from nearby Bolinas to the 230-miles-distant town of Exeter in the Central Valley.

Not surprisingly, conventional distributors such as Banner Fruit Co. range farther afield. According to a survey of nine wholesalers at the Golden Gate Produce Terminal in South San Francisco, their produce comes not only from California but

Arizona, Washington, Texas and Mexico, with distances from farm region to market averaging 942 miles. These distributors supply produce to small- and medium-size grocery stores in the region, including Whole Foods and Mollie Stone's; large chains such as Safeway and Costco manage their own distribution systems. They use semi-trailer trucks that can pack more than 40,000 pounds of food—about 20 times the largest load hauled by a farmer.

Local Versus Imported Food

But how does that translate to carbon dioxide emissions? To find out, I crunched the numbers on five types of produce—apples, oranges, lettuce, greens and squash—with fuel efficiency estimates from the Environmental Protection Agency and Bay Area truck dealers. Factor in carbon emission figures from Argonne National Laboratory, and I had rough carbon footprints for each farmer and wholesaler.

Local farmers won one category, proving more carbon-friendly on squash. While farmers came from cities about an hour's drive from San Francisco, wholesalers had imported their squash through Arizona from Mexico. In these cases, the idea that more food miles equals more fossil fuels appeared to be true.

But wholesalers beat local farmers on the four other produce items, boasting fewer average carbon dioxide emissions per pound of apples, oranges, lettuce and greens. Apple distributors got almost all their apples from Washington's Yakima Valley, about 700 miles away. (Safeway's California stores get Granny Smith apples from Stockton during fall and winter, and from Washington the rest of the year.) While the two local apple farmers traveled one-tenth the distance, their loads averaged less than 700 pounds—and generated six times more carbon dioxide per pound of apples than the semi-trailer trucks.

Local oranges didn't fare much better. Part of the reason is that "conventional" oranges are local, too. Distributors shipped most of their oranges from California's Central Valley, a mere 200 miles from San Francisco and the home of several farmers market vendors. Conventional lettuce and greens came mainly from Arizona and also produced less carbon dioxide during transportation, though by a smaller margin.

A Complicated Question

The Farmers Market's green image was beginning to look a bit tarnished. But no sooner did I finish my calculations than I started to wonder if I had missed some hidden carbon costs. For one, I'd asked the wholesalers how far their produce traveled to the terminal market—but what about the extra leg from the terminal market to the retail store? For that matter, how much

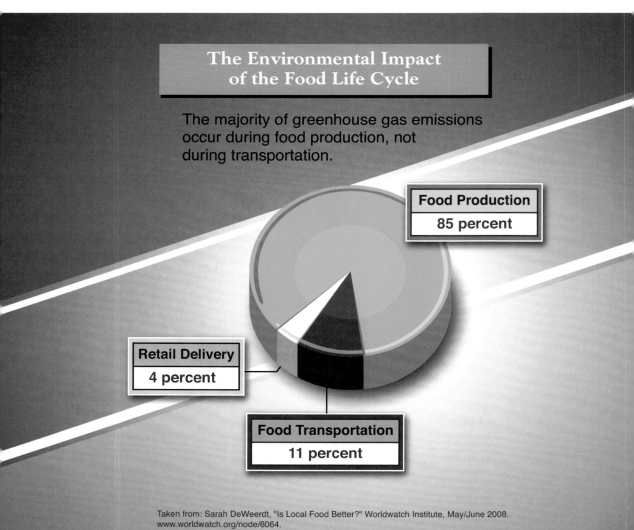

The Environmental Impact of the Food Life Cycle

The majority of greenhouse gas emissions occur during food production, not during transportation.

Food Production
85 percent

Retail Delivery
4 percent

Food Transportation
11 percent

Taken from: Sarah DeWeerdt, "Is Local Food Better?" Worldwatch Institute, May/June 2008.
www.worldwatch.org/node/6064.

carbon dioxide was emitted while consolidating 45,000 pounds of produce from various farms into one semi-trailer truck? And how about the distance traveled by the consumers themselves, whether to the grocery store or to the Farmers Market? What kind of cars did they drive?

Food researchers felt my pain. "There are so many complexities," says Holly Hill, author of a 2008 food miles review for the National Sustainable Agriculture Information Service. "Trying to make those real exact calculations is nearly impossible."

Despite the difficulties, scientists are now devising methods that attempt to calculate every waft of greenhouse gas for a given food product. That means examining a product's entire "life cycle," from fertilization and heating to packaging and storage. Fertilizer production, for example, is an energy-intensive process that can release copious carbon dioxide. And nitrogen fertilizer releases the greenhouse gas nitrous oxide after it is applied to fields. Refrigerating picked fruit for later distribution is another source of carbon dioxide emissions.

Local Is Not Always Better

When scientists look behind the scenes, local food doesn't always come out on top. A 2005 report for the U.K.'s [United Kingdom's] Department for Environment, Food and Rural Affairs (DEFRA) found that growing local tomatoes caused more than three times the carbon dioxide emissions of importing Spanish tomatoes. The culprit was the glasshouse heating required to grow tomatoes locally.

In one of the most high-profile examples, New Zealand researchers reported in 2006 that some of New Zealand's top food exports boasted less energy-intensive production than food produced locally in the U.K., even when the long trip was taken into account. Raising lambs on New Zealand's grassy slopes required four times less energy than U.K. lamb, which relied more heavily on fertilizer, they said. The same pattern held for dairy, which used half as much energy, and apples, which used 60 percent.

"It's lucky I've taken out New Zealand citizenship," says lead investigator and U.K. native Caroline Saunders, who directs the Agribusiness and Economics Research Unit at Lincoln University, and faced criticism from British consumer groups and farmers organizations after the report came out. Saunders argues that storing local food gobbles more energy than shipping, particularly if you want the same products year-round. Even if everyone went local, she says, there's no way that some regions could meet the demand. "I can't see Los Angeles feeding itself within 100 miles," she says.

Other researchers acknowledge the shortcomings of food miles but believe it's still a useful concept for educating the public. It makes consumers think about the ecological consequences of their food choices instead of just considering taste and price, says Gail Feenstra, a food systems analyst at the University of California Sustainable Agriculture Research and Education Program. "Anything that can be done to make people aware of limits to our resources is good," Feenstra says.

Looking at Different Criteria

But Saunders says this kind of "education" could discredit the local food movement when consumers find out food miles can create a misleading picture. "I think if we're going to push simplistic concepts, we've got to have credibility," she says. "Let's think of another one, not food miles."

Scientists are already scrambling for a better answer. The DEFRA report suggests tracking indicators such as the distance flown by air or driven on urban roads per unit of food, which might reflect the damaging effects of food transport (like pollution and traffic congestion) more accurately. Society should also consider the economic and social costs of local food systems, which could hold back the growth of developing nations, argues a 2007 European Science Foundation report on trends in food distribution.

San Francisco Farmers Market representative Julie Cummins agrees that environmentalism shouldn't be the only consideration when buying food. But she argues that going local supports regional agriculture and builds relationships with the people who grow your food. If you're concerned about a particular issue such as pesticide or water use, she says, you can just ask farmers about their agricultural practices—something that's not possible at conventional grocery stores. "It lets you make informed food choices," says Cummins, education director at the Center for Urban Education About Sustainable Agriculture (CUESA), which manages the Ferry Plaza Farmers Market.

The conventional food system can be tough to penetrate. Produce often passes through the hands of brokers before it lands in the grocery store, making it more difficult for customers to find out how an item was grown and transported. "Almost nothing gets done direct anymore," says Pat King, an Oakland-based Fruit and Vegetable Market News officer for the U.S. Department of Agriculture. Some wholesaler employees at the Golden Gate Produce Terminal didn't know exactly where their vegetables were grown, only that they originated somewhere in Mexico.

But local farmers, too, may succumb to the lure of the middleman. In his 2001 study, Pirog found that a regional system with some urban distribution centers produced less carbon dioxide than a purely local system. The local food movement may adopt a system where smaller growers deliver to larger growers, who then bring food into the city, Pirog says. The primary reason local food isn't as efficient is that small farmers "don't have the infrastructure in place like the big guys do," he says.

In the meantime, what's a consumer to do? Food miles don't tell the whole story, and life cycle analyses are too much work for a weekend shopping trip. Cummins sympathizes with the eco-foodie's plight. "It's not a simple thing," she says. "People want to do the best that they can do without pulling their hair out."

I haven't torn out any hair, but my head does hurt a little wondering where to buy my next apple. Pirog's prediction that carbon calculations will eventually become passé—to be replaced with more sophisticated indicators such as water quality impact and geopolitical factors—doesn't help. The next time I go to the Farmers Market, maybe I'll leave my calculator at home.

TWELVE

"Green" Companies Should Be Carefully Evaluated

Janice Podsada

> Janice Podsada is a reporter for the *Hartford Courant* news-
> paper in Hartford, Connecticut. In the following viewpoint
> Podsada discusses the practice of "greenwashing," in which
> companies claim that their products are environmentally
> friendly in order to increase sales. Podsada explains the lack
> of agreement about what makes a product "green" and ques-
> tions some products that are advertised as "green" without
> any proof of good environmental practices. Podsada con-
> cludes that consumers must carefully evaluate any compa-
> ny or product that claims to be "green."

It's non-toxic, biodegradable and all-natural. Its manufacture
is energy-efficient. It's the ultimate in eco-clothing.

The fur coat.

According to the Fur Council of Canada—fur, like organic
lettuce and solar power, is green.

The furs that are green are abundant, and never from endangered species, said Alan Herscovici, executive vice president of
the nonprofit industry group.

Fur farms use leftovers from the human food supply, and the
harvest of wild fur is crucial to maintaining ecological equilib-
rium.

"Too many beavers can cause flooding and too many foxes can decimate the songbird population," Herscovici said.

As for the alternative—synthetic fur—it's made from non-biodegradable petrochemicals.

Green sells. So, whether it's chocolates, eco-travel or a full-length mink or muskrat coat, more manufacturers are labeling their products as environment-friendly or "green" in an effort to broaden appeal and boost sales.

Understanding the "Green" Label

But all that glistens is not green, said Ted Martens with Sustainable Travel International, a nonprofit group that promotes eco-friendly travel.

"Unfortunately, too many people are taking the green name and running with it for marketing purposes," said Martens, the group's director of outreach and development.

Surrounded by all that is verdant, it's no wonder we're confused: Who determines what is green? And how do you evaluate whether a product or service really is green?

"It's a bit of a stretch to say that wearing fur is going to help the environment," said Bruce Cox, executive director of Greenpeace Canada, commenting on the fur council's campaign—www.furisgreen.com. "They present this idea that they are the stewards of the environment. There's a good chance the coat the model is wearing was a farm-raised fur that was electrocuted. I don't think a lot of people actually buy the message."

Is there a soldier of fortune on your gift list?

BAE Systems in Arlington, VA, is developing "green" armaments, including lead-free bullets and a hybrid electric drive system for combat vehicles as part of the U.S. Army's Future Combat Systems program.

"Anybody can make a green claim; it's up to the consumer to understand what that claim means and to decide if they want to do business with that company," said Scot Case, vice president of TerraChoice Environmental Marketing Group, located in Reading, Pa.

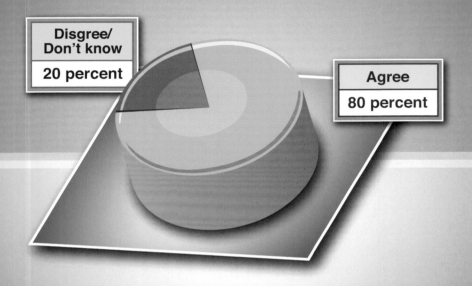

Most Americans Support Green Companies

Agree or disagree: A company's environmental record should be an important factor in deciding whether to buy its products.

Disgree/Don't know

20 percent

Agree

80 percent

Taken from: Patrick O'Driscoll and Elizabeth Weise, "Doing Right Thing Isn't Easy, Even for Those Who Want To," *USA Today*, April 19, 2007.

The Practice of "Greenwashing"

More than 30 million Americans are "true Greens who regularly buy green products," according to Mintel International Group, a Chicago market research company.

As a result, everything from furniture polish to sexual aids (no potentially harmful phthalates) are suddenly turning "green."

Greenwashing—the act of misleading consumers into believing that a company's environmental practices or its product or services are environment-friendly—is pervasive, Case said.

Inaccurate, unsubstantiated and vague claims are common greenwashing ploys, as is the "hidden-trade-off," a marketing strategy that boasts a product's environment-friendly attributes, but fails to mention its drawbacks, "such as an appliance that is said to be energy-efficient, but is full of mercury," Case said.

TerraChoice recently evaluated more than 1,000 widely available consumer products—including appliances, personal products and household cleaners—that purport to be green. Using criteria established by the U.S. Environmental Protection Agency, Consumers Union, Canadian Consumer Affairs

A customer shops at the TerraCycle Green Up Shop in New York. The store features over one hundred green products made from waste materials.

Branch and other agencies, it found that the majority of those products "made claims that are either demonstrably false or that risk misleading intended audiences."

Buyer Beware

"When it comes to these kinds of claims, this is the wild, wild West," Case said.

What's a consumer to do?

The Federal Trade Commission advises consumers to look for specific information. Vague or general claims "may sound warm and fuzzy, but they generally offer little information of value."

Shop for products that carry the EcoLogo or Green Seal, Case said. Since 1988, the Canadian EcoLogo program has certified more than 7,000 products.

"Consumers should not make a purchasing decision based on a green claim unless they understand what that claim means," Case said.

If a product lacks legitimate certification, check the packaging, the company's website or call the manufacturer's toll-free number.

"If they can't explain what the term environmentally friendly means, don't buy the product," he said.

And even if they can explain their terms, buyer beware.

The green marketplace, worth an estimated $200 billion in 2006, is growing, the Mintel Group said. To cash in, some manufacturers are creating their own green standards to convince shoppers that their products are environment-friendly, Case said.

When manufacturers develop their own rules—surprise, surprise —"they tend to meet them," he said.

According to the fur council, to be considered environment-friendly, apparel and accessories should be made from natural materials that are renewable, durable, biodegradable, nontoxic and energy-efficient in its production, use and disposal.

Using that definition, fur is as green as a hybrid car.

"I have been an environmentalist for 15 years," Case said. "And I don't know any environmentalists who wear fur."

Greenness, like beauty, is ultimately in the eye of the beholder.

Good green standards are based on multiple environmental considerations—the impact of the raw materials that go into a product, the environmental impact associated with its manufacture and transport, and its ability to be recycled when it's no longer usable, Case said.

That said, it's up to consumers to decide how green is their intended purchase.

"If you read their definition of green and you agree with it, then buy it."

What You Should Know About Going Green

What Going Green Is

The color green has been associated with environmental and ecological activism in the United States since the 1960s and continues to represent environmentally responsible actions. "Going green" is the term commonly used to describe lifestyle changes that are intended to protect the environment, save energy, reduce pollution, and conserve natural resources like water, land, and trees. "Going green" has no single official definition. It is a flexible concept that describes a wide range of actions that intentionally reduce the impact of humans on Earth. A choice to go green can mean anything from making a small change, such as recycling cans and bottles, to investing in an electric car or installing solar panels on a home.

Facts About Going Green

Every day, people make choices about what they do, how they do it, and what products they use or consume as they go about their lives. As individuals, they may not think that their behavior makes much of a difference in the big picture of environmental awareness. One plastic bag or water bottle thrown in the trash may not seem to matter. Bringing reusable shopping bags from home may seem like too much effort. But even the smallest choices, when combined with the actions of others, can add up to a huge impact on the planet. Consider these facts about the impact that humanity has on Earth's environment:

- Worldwide, the equivalent of almost 270,000 trees is either flushed down toilets or dumped in landfills every day; roughly 10 percent of that total amount is toilet paper.
- Every year, Americans fill enough garbage trucks to stretch from Earth halfway to the moon.
- Every day, Americans produce enough trash to equal the weight of the Empire State Building in New York City.
- Every hour, Americans throw away 2.5 million plastic bottles.
- Every year, roughly 5 percent of all the electricity used in the United States is for "standby power"—the power used by electrical devices such as computers or video game systems that are always on even when not in use; this costs Americans more than $5 billion each year.
- Every year, the average American household uses enough electricity generated by fossil fuels to put more carbon dioxide into the air than two average cars.
- Sixty percent of all paper manufactured in the United States ends up in landfills; only 40 percent is recycled for another use.
- The average American household uses three hundred gallons of water each day, more than twice as much as the average European household.

The green choices people make collectively reduce environmental damage. Going green has an enormous impact on the environment:

- Each year, recycling reduces global warming pollution by the equivalent of removing 39.6 million passenger cars from the road.
- The United States currently recycles 32.5 percent of its waste, compared with about 5 percent in 1970.
- Thirty-one percent of plastic soft drink bottles, 45 percent of aluminum cans, and 67 percent of all major appliances are now recycled in the United States.
- Recycling 1 ton of paper saves the equivalent of 17 trees, 2 barrels of oil, 4,100 kilowatts of energy, 3.2 cubic yards of landfill space, and 60 pounds of air pollution.

- Recycling one ton of glass saves the equivalent of nine gallons of oil.
- Recycling one ton of plastic bags saves the equivalent of seventeen trees and eleven barrels of oil.
- Americans could save more than 16 million trees each year simply by viewing and paying bills online.
- Replacing just five regular lightbulbs with compact flourescent lights (CFL) in every household in the United States would prevent greenhouse gases equivalent to the emissions from nearly 10 million cars.
- Drying laundry on a clothesline instead of in a clothes dryer can reduce the carbon emissions of the laundry process by up to 90 percent.

What You Should Do About Going Green

If you are interested in going green, you will find many different ways to start. Your family may already be making green choices, either on purpose or without knowing it. For example, carpooling with other families or using public transportation are green choices. Many cities across the United States now provide household recycling along with regular garbage pickup. Services like this make it easier for people to go green without a lot of extra effort. If you want to do more, think about your habits and which changes you could make to become more environmentally conscious. Keep in mind that if you try to make a lot of big changes all at once, you are more likely to become overwhelmed and give up. Try starting with one small change that you can develop into a habit over time. Then you can add more small changes, one or two at a time, as you get used to making different choices. Here are some ideas for what you can do to go green:

- Recycle as much trash and waste as possible, including paper, glass, plastic, and aluminum cans; you can find information on recycling centers near you by entering your zip code at www.thedailygreen.com.
- Reduce the number of things you purchase or acquire, and live with less "stuff."
- Buy or take only what you need, and use all of it; for example, when you are at a restaurant take only as many ketchup packets or napkins as you will use, to prevent the extras from becoming waste.
- Find ways to reuse items rather than throwing them away, either by repairing those that are broken or torn or finding creative new uses for old items.
- Conserve energy as much as possible by reducing the amount of electricity, gas, and hot water that you use.
- Buy food and other items that are produced locally, to limit the amount of energy that is used in the transportation of

goods for sale; you can find out about farmers' markets near you by entering your zip code at www.thedailygreen.com.

- Buy environmentally friendly products or products that are made from recycled materials; you can find information on green alternatives at www.goodguide.com, a directory of thousands of products, including food, toys, and household items.
- Find ways to reduce your use of water; for example, when brushing your teeth, turn the water off until you need it.
- Bring your own reusable bags when shopping so you do not have to take plastic or paper bags from stores.
- Turn the lights off when you leave a room.
- Turn off televisions, computers, and video game systems when you are not using them.
- Unplug appliances such as phone and video game controller chargers until you need to use them.
- Instead of turning up the heat in the winter, try putting on a sweater to warm yourself rather than increasing the heat for your entire home.

If you live in a home where your family has control over the hot water heater or thermostat, talk to your parents or the other adults you live with about dialing down to save energy. Lowering the thermostat on your hot water heater to 120 degrees will conserve energy while still providing hot water. Turning down the furnace thermostat by even one or two degrees will conserve energy and save money for your family. You can also talk about changing some of the regular lightbulbs in your home to compact fluorescent lights (CFLs). CFL bulbs last much longer and use much less energy than traditional incandescent bulbs, which will also save money for your family over time.

The editors have compiled the following list of organizations concerned with the issues debated in this book. The descriptions are derived from materials provided by the organizations. All have publications or information available for interested readers. The list was compiled on the date of publication of the present volume; the information provided here may change. Be aware that many organizations take several weeks or longer to respond to inquiries, so allow as much time as possible for the receipt of requested materials.

American Forests
PO Box 2000, Washington, DC 20013
(202) 737-1944
e-mail: info@amfor.org
Web site: www.americanforests.org

Founded in 1875, American Forests is one of the oldest nonprofit citizens' conservation organizations in the United States. The organization's mission is "to grow a healthier world" through healthy forest ecosystems in every community. American Forests works with individuals, community groups, educators, businesses, and all levels of government. Its Web site includes current news, an archive of *American Forests* magazine, information about current and past projects, a resource library, and a free monthly e-mail newsletter.

Earth911
1375 N. Scottsdale Rd., Ste. 360
Scottsdale, AZ 85257
(480) 889-2650
Web site: http://earth911.com

Earth911 promotes the message that recycling is not only easy, but it can also be fun. The mission of Earth911 is to educate people and businesses about the concepts of "reduce, reuse, and recycle." Its Web site features a searchable database listing more than one-hundred thousand recycling locations across the country that handle all types of recyclable materials. The Web site also provides a "Recycling 101" tutorial and an extensive news and lifestyle resource library, including a weekly e-mail newsletter.

Eco-Cycle
PO Box 19006, Boulder, CO 80308
e-mail: recycle@ecocycle.org
Web site: www.ecocycle.org

Eco-Cycle is a national nonprofit recycling organization that is committed to transforming society's "throw-away ethic" into environmentally responsible stewardship through the concepts and practices of the zero waste philosophy. It provides community education programs and recycling services for communities and businesses. Its Web site includes an online newsletter as well as extensive information on the Zero Waste movement and recycling at home, work, and school.

Environmental Protection Agency (EPA)
Ariel Rios Bldg., 1200 Pennsylvania Ave. NW
Washington, DC 20460
(202) 272-0167
Web site: www.epa.gov

The EPA is an agency of the U.S. federal government. Its mission is to protect human health and to safeguard the natural environment. The EPA is responsible for writing and enforcing regulations and national standards on environmental issues and practices. Its Web site provides extensive information about EPA activities and the environmental issues that fall under EPA jurisdiction. A special section for students and educators provides educational materials on environmental protection, conservation, and more.

Focus the Nation
240 N. Broadway, Ste. 212
Portland, OR 97227

(503) 224-9440
e-mail: info@focusthenation.org
Web site: www.focusthenation.org

Focus the Nation is a national nonprofit organization that focuses on climate change and green energy. The organization is committed to empowering young people with leadership, education, and civic engagement opportunities. Its Web site provides information about current and past programs as well as the Focus Roots Fellowship, a competitive annual series of ten-thousand-dollar grants awarded to the most innovative and creative young climate leaders.

Friends of the Earth
1100 Fifteenth St. NW, 11th Fl.
Washington, DC 20005
(202) 783-7400
Web site: www.foe.org

Friends of the Earth is a worldwide network of grassroots organizations united to protect the environment and encourage green living. Its Web site contains information about topics such as global warming, air and water quality, healthy living, clean energy, and updates on current events and programs. An online media center provides access to an archive of newsletters, magazines, and other publications.

Global Footprint Network
312 Clay St., Ste. 300
Oakland, CA 94607
(510) 839-8879
Web site: www.footprintnetwork.org

The Global Footprint Network is a global scientific organization that focuses on measuring the environmental impact of humans and the rate of consumption of Earth's natural resources. Its Web site includes extensive information about the ecological footprint concept and the scientific methods of measuring human impact on the environment. An online resource library provides access to case studies, events, interviews, and related publications. The site's footprint calculator helps people measure the environmental impact of their own actions.

Greenpeace
702 H St. NW, Ste. 300
Washington, DC 20001
(202) 462-1177
e-mail: info@wdc.greenpeace.org
Web site: www.greenpeace.org

Greenpeace is an environmental activism organization that encourages the formation of global solutions to environmental problems. Its Web site provides extensive information about Greenpeace actions on a range of green issues, such as global warming, clean energy, and the protection of Earth's oceans and forests. A multimedia library of photos and videos is also available on the Web site.

LocalHarvest
PO Box 1292
Santa Cruz, CA 95061
(831) 515-5602
Web site: www.localharvest.org

LocalHarvest maintains one of the largest and most comprehensive directories of small farms, farmers' markets, and community-supported agriculture programs in the nation. Its Web site features blogs, community discussion forums, a food and farming events calendar, a search function that helps people find sources of locally grown food, and an online store that helps small farms market their products.

Mother Nature Network (MNN)
Web site: www.mnn.com

The goal of the MNN is to "improve your world" by providing extensive resources through its Web site and Web-based community. Its Web site is divided into eight different sections, each focused on a different topic related to green living. Also available on the Web site is a free e-mail newsletter, news on current events and government actions related to environmental issues, and a glossary of eco-related terms.

National Recycling Coalition (NRC)
805 Fifteenth St. NW, Ste. 425
Washington, DC 20005
(202) 789-1430
Web site: www.nrc-recycle.org

The NRC is a nonprofit advocacy group that promotes waste reduction, reuse, composting, and recycling in North America. Its Web site provides information about state and regional recycling programs and news related to recycling and waste reduction/management efforts.

Natural Resources Defense Council (NRDC)
40 W. Twentieth St.
New York, NY 10011
(212) 727-2700
e-mail: nrdcinfo@nrdc.org
Web site: www.nrdc.org

The NRDC is a grassroots environmental action group that works to protect wildlife, ensure a healthy environment, reduce global warming, and promote clean energy. Its Web site provides information about environmental concerns, U.S. environmental laws and policies, environmental justice, green living, and green business practices. An online activist network provides information about current action campaigns and tools for individual action.

350.org
The David Brower Center, Ste. 340
Berkeley, CA 94704
(510) 250-7860
Web site: www.350.org

350.org is a global action network uniting more than two hundred member organizations around the world. Through grassroots organizing and activism, the network promotes the creation and adoption of international solutions to reduce the carbon emissions that cause global warming. The network takes its name from 350ppm (parts per million), the number representing the maximum amount of carbon dioxide that can safely exist in Earth's atmosphere. Its Web site includes action ideas and organizing plans, downloadable posters, fliers, stencils, and a special section for youth activism.

Union of Concerned Scientists
2 Brattle Sq.
Cambridge, MA 02238
(617) 547-5552
Web site: www.ucsusa.org

The Union of Concerned Scientists is a nonprofit alliance of scientists, teachers, students, and members of the general public. The group uses independent scientific research and activism to encourage changes in government policy, corporate practices, and consumer choices that support clean energy and a healthier environment. Its Web site includes information on current and pending legislation related to environmental issues and an extensive resource library of fact sheets, letters, position papers, publications, news stories, and more.

WorldChanging
1301 First Ave., Ste. 301
Seattle, WA 98101
Web site: www.worldchanging.com

WorldChanging is a nonprofit worldwide network of media professionals and organizations interested in encouraging innovative solutions to environmental problems. Its Web site includes a large collection of news articles and information about models and ideas for creating a green future through renewable energy, improved building practices, transportation, and communication.

BIBLIOGRAPHY

Books

Ed Begley Jr., *Living Like Ed: A Guide to the Eco-friendly Life*. New York: Clarkson Potter, 2008.

Kevin Danaher, *Building the Green Economy: Success Stories from the Grassroots*. Sausalito, CA: PoliPointPress, 2007.

Brangien Davis and Katharine Wroth, eds., *Wake Up and Smell the Planet: The Nonpompous, Nonpreachy Grist Guide to Greening Your Day*. Seattle, WA: Skipstone, 2007.

Thomas L. Friedman, *Hot, Flat, and Crowded: Why We Need a Green Revolution—and How It Can Renew America*. New York: Farrar, Straus and Giroux, 2008.

Al Gore, *Earth in the Balance: Ecology and the Human Spirit*. New York: Rodale, 2006.

Greg Horn, *Living Green: A Practical Guide for Simple Sustainability*. Topanga, CA: Freedom Press, 2006.

Yvonne Jeffery, Liz Barclay, and Michael Grosvenor, *Green Living for Dummies*. Indianapolis, IN: Wiley, 2008.

Vaclav Klaus, *Blue Planet in Green Shackles: What Is Endangered, Climate or Freedom?* Washington, DC: Competitive Enterprise Institute, 2007.

Steven Milloy, *Green Hell: How Environmentalists Plan to Control Your Life and What You Can Do to Stop Them*. Washington, DC: Regnery, 2009.

Laura Pritchett, ed., *Going Green: True Tales from Gleaners, Scavengers, and Dumpster Divers*. Norman: University of Oklahoma Press, 2009.

Trish Riley, *The Complete Idiot's Guide to Green Living*. New York: Alpha, 2007.

Periodicals and Internet Sources

Jerry Adler, "Going Green: With Windmills, Low-Energy Homes, New Forms of Recycling and Fuel-Efficient Cars,

Americans Are Taking Conservation into Their Own Hands," *Newsweek*, July 17, 2006.

Nicole Bradford, "Necessity, Not a 'Green Movement,' Drove Past Generations to Conservation, Efficiency," *Houston Business Journal*, November 28, 2008.

Robert Bryce, "Five Myths About Green Energy," *Washington Post*, April 25, 2010.

Dave Cherry, "No Excuse for Not Going 'Green,'" AZCentral, October 18, 2007. www.azcentral.com/12news/consumer/articles/2007/10/18/20071018GREENexcusesSCRIPT10182007-CR.html.

Sally Deneen, "How to Recycle Practically Anything," *E*, 2009. www.emagazine.com/view/?3172.

Collin Dunn, "Eating Local Food: The Movement, Locavores, and More," Treehugger, March 6, 2008. www.treehugger.com/files/2008/03/green-basics-eat-local-food.php.

John Feffer, "The Challenge Facing Local Food," *Salon*, January 18, 2007. www.salon.com/life/food/eat_drink/2007/01/18/eat_local/index.html.

Pallavi Gogoi, "The Rise of the 'Locavore,'" *Bloomberg BusinessWeek*, May 20, 2008. www.businessweek.com/bwdaily/dnflash/content/may2008/db20080520_920283.htm.

Miguel A. Guanipa, "The Green Religion," *American Thinker*, October 5, 2008.

Kristen Hampshire, Kyle Swenson, Beth Stallings, and Lynne Thompson, "The Greendustry," *Inside Business*, August 2008.

Eviana Hartman, "Going, Going, Green," *Washington Post*, August 6, 2006.

Mark Hertsgaard, "Green Goes Grassroots: The Environmental Movement Today," *Nation*, July 31, 2006.

William P. Hoar, "Another Great Green Scam," *New American*, December 21, 2009.

Edward Iwata, "Companies Discover Going Green Pays Off," *USA Today*, May 22, 2008.

Paul Johnson, "Going Green Doesn't Have to Mean Going Broke," *Boston Globe*, January 24, 2009.

Rich Karlgaard, "Green Greens Versus Red Greens," *Forbes*, June 18, 2007.

Brian Kelly, "Going Green Is Good Business," *U.S. News & World Report*, April 1, 2010.

Linsey Knerl, "4 Reasons Why Green Is Good, but Isn't Always Better," Wise Bread, August 24, 2008. www.wisebread.com/4-reasons-why-green-is-good-but-isnt-always-better.

Tara Lohan, "The Great Plastic Bag Plague," AlterNet, September 5, 2007. www.alternet.org/environment/61607/the_great_plastic_bag_plague.

Jason Mark, "Beyond the Green Niche," *Progressive*, February 2010.

Andrew Martin, "If It's Fresh and Local, Is It Always Greener?" *New York Times*, December 9, 2007.

David Morris, "Green, at Any Cost?" *Irregular*, February 18, 2009. www.theirregular.com/news/2009/0218/op_ed/013.html.

Jack Neff, "Earth Day Is 40 Years Old: What Headway Have We Made? *Ad Age* Tallies Up What's Come of Industry's Green Movement," *Advertising Age*, April 19, 2010.

NPR, "Beyond Recycling: Getting to 'Zero Waste,'" March 28, 2008. www.npr.org/templates/story/story.php?storyId=89169980.

Bill Nye, "Food Waste," Gaiam Life, 2010. http://life.gaiam.com/gaiam/p/Stuff-Happens-with-Bill-Nye-How-to-Fight-Food-Waste.html.

Sara Ost, "Fail: 20 Infamous 'Green Innovations' That Aren't," WebEcoist, October 20, 2008. http://webecoist.com/2008/10/20/failed-green-technologies-designs-and-innovations.

Ashley Phillips, "Will Going Green Lose Some Gusto?" ABC News, July 12, 2007. http://abcnews.go.com/technology/globalwarming/Story?id=3366763.

Tom Philpott, "The Eat-Local Backlash: If Buying Locally Isn't the Answer, Then What Is?" *Grist*, August 16, 2007. www.grist.org/article/eatlocal.

Bernie Reeves, "Attack of the Green Meanies," *American Thinker*, September 14, 2009.

Marc Sheppard, "Save the Children (from Global Warming Propaganda)," *American Thinker*, February 5, 2009.

Dashka Slater, "The Future of Garbage," *Sierra*, March/April 2010.

Alex Nicolai Steffen, "The Next Green Revolution," *Wired*, May 2006. www.wired.com/wired/archive/14.05/green.html.

Alex Williams, "Buying into the Green Movement," *New York Times*, July 1, 2007.

Deborah Zabarenko, "Do Food Miles Affect Global Warming?" *USA Today*, October 18, 2007.

PICTURE CREDITS